Living and Dying with Dogs

Duke Miller

D1707486

booktrope

Booktrope Editions
Seattle, WA 2013

Cover Design by Greg Simanson

Edited by Peter Sheehy

This is a work of fiction. Names, characters, places, brands, media, and incidents are either the product of the author's imagination or are used fictitiously. Any resemblance to similarly named places or to persons living or deceased is unintentional.

PRINT ISBN 978-1-62015-175-4

EPUB ISBN 978-1-62015-271-3

Library of Congress Control Number: 2014900261

ACKNOWLEDGMENTS

This is for Tres and Marsh, who are my life and, of course, my mom and dad. My heart is full of many others and I owe them more than they will ever know. Thanks to my buddy and editor, Pete "Knucks" Sheehy. Finally, my dogs: they teach me what we have lost. It is in their eyes and silent messages.

CONTENTS

Prologue..7

Giant Vanishing Bees..11

Body Surfing in El Salvador...................................14

Nobody Knows..17

The Brigadier General and All That Is Golden........19

Alona and the Scented Garden..............................21

Stanley Loves Humphrey Bogart..........................25

A Very Small Moment...28

The Man Who Couldn't Come...............................33

The Leper Colony...39

In My Medical Opinion...47

Death to the Monkeys...52

Christian Girls Do Other Things...........................54

The Public Health of Murder................................57

The Ménage a' Trois of Passports.........................64

The Ghost Reschedules...66

Death and Garbage on the International Art Market........73

Two Bullets...76

Remembering...80

The Heat Novel..85

Tortilla Mouth...93

Half a Blackbird..97

My Insignificant Relationship with Stars............102

Peace in the Jungle 108

The Eyes of Man and Dog 112

Death Spreads Her Legs 115

The Horse Loving Refugee Poet of Hollywood 118

Eating Breakfast in the Third World 126

She Saw Jesus Standing There 129

The Bus at the End of My Universe 130

Epilogue: The Man with the Golden Skins 135

"If extreme events inform one's writing, then I think I have enough information."

—DM

PROLOGUE

I AWOKE IN PAIN at the bottom of a cliff. I thought my back was broken, maybe my neck. I couldn't breathe, hear, or talk. My bones were silent. The dogs were voiceless; throwing their heads back with open jaws and mutely howling about unexpected change.

Two striking women have always been a mystery to me: Francesca Woodman and Elizabeth Hartman, they both jumped to their deaths, tortured by art and men. Everything had been there for them, but for some reason it wasn't enough and then the high wind offered a short journey.

I carry them around with me like unlucky coins in my pocket.

I think about the pair when I see a handsome black man touching a white girl's face or when I'm in a museum and I see a scratchy black and white photo of a breast or leg wrapped in sheer plastic. They were both talented artists, but they thought of themselves as defective when others turned them over and inspected the pores of their skin. So they checked out, but why jump? Why not drugs, a gun, a razor, or gas?

When I hit the first ledge, I found out. A head crushed by stone goes instantly to nothing: no pain, no god, just black, as if one were sitting in a movie theatre hit by a power outage.

As I lay there, the rocks were grinding me into dust and then the title and voice of this book came to me. They were competing with my need to die properly at the base of the cliff, but I didn't die.

I crawled back up telling myself that I could make it as my dogs flew around me with dog capes fluttering in the air.

I started writing in my mind that night in the hospital: blood for ink, air for pages, past for honesty.

"Living and Dying with Dogs" is not a novel or a collection of short stories. It's a lack of character study; a kind of long, sad poem written in constantly updating akashic sentences that have evolved into skins or life maps that hang in the closet of my heart.

It's about how I die.

Paint by the numbers and with each pigment, you add what I was and what I am and maybe what I hope to be. The images are the people I left behind. I don't want to take them with me into oblivion at the bottom of some new cliff just ahead.

You take these emotions, these characters. If you don't mind, let them loiter in your heart for a few days or longer. Most of them had a pretty rough time. They'd like that.

The voice you will be hearing bets on the dying, fiddles with autofellatio, smokes opium, takes amphetamines, brushes against pedophilia, leaves people for dead, drinks too much, says things he shouldn't, aborts babies, disappoints lovers, kicks the dying, weeps uncontrollably, causes his tortured lover to go to jail, can't sleep, lies, and looks upon orgasms as a sort of Sasquatch of the lower realms.

But other than that, he's a good guy and if you could sit with him over a beer or a joint, you'd probably like him. Think of him as a prehistoric creature, swishing his tail across the yellow grass of a savanna; oblivious to the world around him, but rising up like a primordial freeway sign pointing the way towards the unfinished off ramp.

Which raises the ancient questions of this poem: Can a person care and not care at the same time? Why do good people do bad things? Why do bad people do good things?

This book is a series of textual distortions pulled from my leather shoulder bag; neither history nor confession. The stories whisper at night and tell about regrets and bodies decomposing.

War and old lovers have set my stage.

Am I an idiot? Probably, but I'm a lousy judge. Judgment is a problem in this world. Just ask my suicide twins, Woodman and Hartman.

My leather bag is my partner. An old Quiche Indian made it for me in the village of Totonicapán and then after years of being battered the bag finally gave up and wilted. It is sad to see leather droop and shrivel like male genitalia. So I went back. The old man was unchanged, still sitting at his bench waiting for Kukulkan to return.

Mayan myth slows the clock ticking on the faces of Guatemalan Indians.

In a few days I got my new bag; a perfect copy. I count on the bag. It is my fourth hand.

You are in the stories. You don't know it, but you're there. I can hear you speaking an obscure language into your lover's ear. You are making a case for a gentle touch and you are lucky. You and I share the same oxygen like a pair of joyful astronauts hyperventilating on the horizon of Ganymede.

I once met a young Bosnian woman in Sarajevo who told me that there "was nothing like love in Sarajevo during the siege." All the joy and sadness in the world enriched her eyes. They shone like two tears of blue obsidian.

She picked up the phone one day in Australia and answered a call from a Bosnian soldier fighting the Serbs. It was a wrong number, but he explained he was calling from Sarajevo. Over the days they talked on the phone and soon they fell in love with the sound of each other's voice.

The young woman decided to leave her safe, good life behind. She made the long trip to Sarajevo to be with the soldier. Standing atop Mt. Igman, she looked down at the broken city. Slowly she made her way along the slopes and entered the little house where the tunnel under the airstrip began. She stooped and crawled in the zigzagging passage way and finally made it through the front lines.

War became the view out her window. Instead of tending flower boxes, she watered sniper victims.

Her life was defined by her love for the soldier and the fight against the Serbs. I don't know what happened to her, but I believe she was totally alive during those days in a way that is unfamiliar to most people.

The tune she played still haunts me.

Our senses flourish when we risk greatly and the passing days take on a romantic quality that holds us like the embraces of a restless lover. We compartmentalize to survive upon hellish ground. Pain gets delayed if we have the time and space.

If we are lucky, we stand on the other side of the river gasping for air, away from the snakes. The breaths of the living are opportunities that the dead have given up and our lungs were once the same. How can we forget?

Things were terrible, but they define us in a way that is unique and separate us at the end. We have nothing else and we surely have not much to lose when we finally arrive.

That was exactly the way I felt at the bottom of the 60-foot cliff.

It was almost dark and along the periphery he noticed a dog chewing on a hand. The sight had almost no impact on him. Dogs eating the carrion flesh of human beings were minor visions and totally understandable. Excited birds, insects, cats, feral dogs, pissing microbes—all things feasted. The stench was a bonus. His flashlight went out and then a woman grabbed his ankle and wouldn't let go. She tried to pull him down into the pile of bodies where she lay near death. Time was being squeezed by a metal press and his panicked form began to lose its balance on the edge of thirty seconds. Her fingernails ripped into his skin. He kicked her in the head with his other foot. She held on. He stepped on her arm and finally she let go. As he reached the top of the pile he looked back at her and she vomited. The other dying congratulated her. None were ready to concede the ground where they waited. The almost dead were critics and quick to take offense. They had nothing to lose as they confronted well-meaning, but ignorant people in the most brutal way. The moon rolled down the volcano and it shone upon an open field with 10,000 dead who didn't care about dogs or footfalls or the dying. He walked upon the dead to get to his tent and none of them seemed to mind. They were beyond such considerations and were without judgment, content to lay in the darkened crevices of unused nightmares. The dead presented fewer problems than the dying and he acted accordingly.

THAILAND

GIANT VANISHING BEES

I FIGURED TO LIVE in a Khlong Toei whorehouse. It was located on Soi 22 off Sukhumvit. About thirty prostitutes had hurt rooms there. It was a large wet wooden structure built in the old style. My place was right beside the little alley that was the main entrance. I saw everybody coming and going. They didn't walk, but seemed to slowly float and buzz through a solid shadow of low, lost days.

Maybe they had VD, or something more mysterious. Whatever the truth, they were like giant vanishing bees. The girls were just starting to hear about HIV/AIDS and hadn't made the connection to dirty needles and unprotected sex. Nature was anonymously attacking them and their doubts sprouted and grew without the sun.

My Thai was good and I tried to be sociable. Some of the girls were nice and others despised me. I saw girls arguing with each other and men hitting the girls and girls nodding off on drugs and girls sick in bed.

A crowd watched one evening when the Bangkok body snatchers carried a dead girl out of the whorehouse next to mine. She was stretched out on a piece of corrugated tin that curved downward with her weight. The dead were picked up by kind hearted people racing around town trying to earn Buddhist merit.

I saw the girl in the pooling darkness and she looked like karma was dripping out of her mouth. The body snatcher bent over and mopped it up with a rag. He'd squeeze the cloth out later into a metal pan and consume it. The neon lights of the alley blinked across my face as the white pickup with the dead girl in the bed slowly moved away.

A prostitute standing beside me said, "Having good time?"

"No," I answered.

"It not matter," she smiled, taking my hand for all that it was worth. "She my friend, we sisters."

Life seemed to revolve around cleanliness in my new home. The prostitutes bathed every day on the little wooden walkways that connected our rooms.

Dressed in cheap lungis they scooped rain water out of big jars. Without makeup they were like pale white animals gathering in virgin woods. Their feet were delicate and narrow. They took turns washing each other's hair in the spotty sunshine and I felt like a man recovering from paralysis as I looked upon the purity of their movements.

I got to know a Muslim and her roommate from Ka Samet. The Muslim girl had a beauty mole on her chin and she would come in late at night after dancing at one of the clubs. Her skin was like a royal procession of silk that stretched from her toes to her nose, but she was depressed and I couldn't take my eyes off her.

Sometimes she would cry and tell me about her family. She was born into a ready-made tragedy. Her mother died in childbirth, while her father disappeared at sea. A mean aunt finally sold her to a rich family from Chiang Mai. After a few years she escaped to Bangkok where she got a job dancing almost naked on a bar top while old men raped her in their minds.

When I was tired, I'd lay my head on her breast and listen to the weak call of her heart from when she was a small child. The beat was monotone and not a symphony. It came to me on the wings of an injured bird from the south.

I worried that maybe her heartbeat was going to drop off into nothing. She was only twenty, too young to have a vital organ tumbling from the sky.

She seemed content with me and would fall asleep on my bed while I wrote bad poetry at a small desk. I was taking Captagon pills to stay awake. I didn't want to miss anything in the whorehouse.

A big water rat used to crawl across the rafters in the room. He became my mascot. A few of the prostitutes would sometimes stop by my window and look in and laugh at me. "Why are you feeding that rat?" they'd giggle. His name was General Wash and he ate cheese and noodles out of my hand. "He's not a rat. He's a dog."

Eventually I left when one of the girls accused me of using heroin. I didn't need that kind of rumor. Although there was plenty of opportunity to use in the house, I'd decided not to stick needles into my arm. The opium had been bad enough.

On my last night the Muslim girl and I went out for fish soup. She said that she would miss me. "Please, you come back. Find me...I here."

The long shot in her voice sailed past me, but as we talked, a life together somehow seemed possible.

She told me about a hidden beach and how we could build a first-rate hut that would protect us from the rain and the beasts of the world. She would catch fish just like her dead father and we would sleep on the sand, covered in soft green breezes. I left her with that hope, and her lips were tight, as she shook her head no to a new dress.

I never returned to find her among the thousands of prostitutes clogging the alleys of Khlong Toei. The best I could do was to carry her in my heart several times around the world.

At night I'd feel her inside me, hanging onto the rise and fall of my breath like she was riding the ocean waves in search of fish to nourish our entwined flesh.

These were some of the most thoughtful days of my life. It had something to do with being a voyeur of horrific pain masquerading as pleasure. Part of being human was laying a veneer on the truth so we could keep on living. Without the lie, I came to understand that some of us would crawl into a corner and die.

Maybe that was why I left the girl with the hope that one day we would be together on a secret beach. It turned out to be bullshit, but maybe it sustained her for a few days, just like it sustained me for a few years.

He was young and trying to make a name for himself in the insurance business. He wanted to be the Empire State Building of health and accident. Let's see here... Okay, now this is just a simple medical history form that we need to fill out before we process your application. He slid it across the table like my will and left the room searching for money down the hall. For some reason I decided to tell the truth, always a risky move. I began to fill in the blanks and check the boxes: malaria (three discreet cases), dengue fever (eyes bled), typhoid, cholera, intractable parasites, tapeworms, hookworms, asthma, stomach ulcers, jungle rashes and rots, various broken bones and fractures, concussions (two), cut eyeball (vision impairment), toxic neuritis (tequila, mostly), aortal heart fibrillation (rockets), syphilis (fiancé gave it to me although she denies it) and chronic back pain (fell sixty feet off cliff while worrying about my dog). Not only did I get turned down, but so did everyone else in the small refugee office where I worked. The insurance company figured the other staff must have caught something from me. I was a walking epidemic similar to millions of rats running through the streets of downtown San Antonio infecting crying babies and old women on social security. I was the Dark Ages come to destroy the dreamy insurance castles of Texas

EL SALVADOR

BODY SURFING IN EL SALVADOR

BODY SURFING IN EL SALVADOR was one of my more pleasant pastimes. On this particular day, I was on an isolated beach one could only reach by hiking through the jungle for an hour. The path was difficult and well off the main highway.

I liked the beach since there was a rock formation that looked like an Alpha Bull flopping around roaring at the sea. The water was warm. I was catching good waves, six feet high all the way to the beach and if there was ever a moment when I was happy, it was then.

Everything changed though, as it always does. On my right appeared the body of a man. We rode the same wave most of the way into shore.

I got out and sat watching him being dragged in and out by the surf. Finally, he got hung on the sand. A few barnacles had attached themselves to his bloated body and I struggled to pull him farther onto the beach.

The back of his head had been blown out by a gun shot. He looked to be a student or maybe a farmer. It was hard to tell. He had been in the water long enough for his skin to have turned white and putrid like one of the thousands of ghosts walking the countryside.

I went to get some food from my bag. The coconut looked good and I took it back down to the body. I began to make up a story about the dead man and then he opened his eyes and corrected what I was thinking.

I offered him a sip of my coconut. The stout breeze from the sea filled his lungs. He whispered no thanks on the coconut.

He told me he had a family and had been working on a union project to organize the docks in Acajutla. The big transport and shipping owners had taken offense and since this was the season for taking offense, they had picked him up one night and taken him down to the sea and killed him.

His executioners were known to him. They weren't friends, but he had seen them in the neighborhood where he lived.

Before they shot him they told him they wouldn't hurt his family. He thanked them for that and then he put his head down and they murdered him and pushed his body over the ledge. He fell upon the rocks and lay there, arms stretched, like Jesus without the second chance.

Eventually high tide floated him out into the current and he began to yo-yo along the coastline. For a few days he passed the same land formations, back and forth, and finally the sea made up its mind and pushed him to Alpha Bull beach and me.

I offered him another sip of my coconut. He declined for a second time. He asked me to please close his eyes for him. They were stinging from the salt in the water. I reached my hand down and did as he asked.

We talked for a few more minutes as he rested within the darkness of his closed eyes and then the tide began to tickle his feet like his children used to do when he slept. Slowly the water came up and the waves took him out.

A few hours later a man with a machete and an old rifle came walking down the beach. He asked me if I had seen a body. I told him no.

He said he was searching for his friend and that some men with guns had taken him from his home a few nights ago and he had heard from a fisherman about a body in the surf. I told him I couldn't help him and then he said thanks and walked on down the beach.

I decided to spend the night. I gathered some wood from the jungle and got up into one of the caves. As I sat near the fire I listened for anyone who might be calling to me from the sea, but I only heard the wind and the sounds of madness screaming down the sides of volcanoes from San Salvador.

I supposed I should have told the man with the machete and the old rifle how I had shut the eyelids of his friend there on the beach, but my courage failed me.

I took the twice rejected coconut and broke it on a rock and ate my supper.

I am a common man. Like everyone else I find that sunshine can put me in an expansive mood. The pulsing waves often help me discover hidden alternatives to trouble. Once I was resting in the sunshine on the steps of a warehouse in Rwanda and the young son of a mass murderer walked up to me and said are you freaking out? I said no, I am visualizing the chemical properties of quicklime as it decomposes human flesh. The fat teenager said that's cool man, as he walked away surrounded by a bunch of drunks looking for work. They laughed and pointed at me. Another time I was sitting in the sunlight on a fallen tree near the village of Rus Rus on the Nicaraguan border. My Indian companion Stanley was with me and we both had our shoes off. Our feet were fighting fungus along the frontlines of our toes. A man came out of the jungle dressed in mismatched fatigues. He asked me what I was doing. I told him I was sunning my feet and thinking about how to manipulate the price of rice. He said I want to tell you a story. I said fine. He then began, I am from Louisiana and I want to see democracy sweep the earth like a broom. Then he goes on about how the Contras are the moral equivalent of the founding fathers. That seemed like a very strange idea to me. About a month later, I was in Tegucigalpa watching American T.V. news. Ronald Reagan came on the air and said that the Contras were the moral equivalent of the founding fathers. I thought back to the man who said he was from Louisiana and how Ronald Reagan was an actor and then I decided I had met Ronald Reagan near the CIA supported village of Rus Rus. I have noticed that hanging around in the sunshine is like being caught up in a crowded procession that rapidly moves through smoke and colored dust. You get to meet individuals who have god-like powers over the living. They are covered in mud or wear red ties. Thousands die in their wake. The light from the sun is a juggernaut and I sometimes think that Albert Einstein is sending me secret itineraries written in lemon juice.

HONDURAS

NOBODY KNOWS

THE LETTER RESTS IN PERIPHERAL VISION instead of an envelope. It comes from the side silently like the sound of paper in a mailbox. The friend of a lover delivers it in slow motion through the hot air of a stuffy bureau in a polluted city filled with refugees. Time pushes it along like hands above an outdated conveyor belt and instead of stamps it is pressed with medical, distant moments.

The letter has survived the storm over the Atlantic and finally arrives in an office full of concerned people, political people trying to make the war better.

How does one make war better?

The face of Pamela smiles and then disappears out the door with barely a word. A hand unfolds the pressed, rough paper of the letter and shows: I am waiting for them to take me into the operating room. I am writing this from my bed. My hair has been cut away from where they will make the incision. I am sad for that. I feel you touching my hair now, gently passing your fingers over my face. The drugs are very good here and I have no pain.

Felipe is still in Thailand. We ended poorly. Claudette and Brigitte are in Ethiopia working on the famine.

I have given this letter to my friend, Pamela. She was in the Paris office a few weeks ago and told me she had met you in El Salvador. Are you still in Honduras? If you are, she said she would find you. Maybe if things go well with my tumor, I will come to Central America.

I started to get sick three months after Bali. I am afraid I am not so pretty right now. The doctors are unsure what will happen. I want you to know that I love you. If I am unlucky, please remember me and remember our time together. At night I can hear our train pass by. Love, Marivel.

The letter is opened and closed a million times as it imprints upon the heart. Can a letter cure cancer? Can words build a blue-eyed doctor with bobbed, blonde hair to sit on a new beach beside a reliable sea?

The letter is soft resurrection and the words are the genetic code of her body enclosing my presence in the office. No one really knows but the two of us and the secret will travel on our slow train, moving toward the sea, lost in the night.

On one side of the road there were a bit less than one million refugees. They were dying in misery and clustered together like swirling wreckage upon the sea. The other side was relatively empty, except for the stacks of bodies or lines of bodies or the occasional single body. As I drove down the road I would sometimes have to stop and let a man or woman crawl on their hands and knees to get to the other side. Sometimes whole families would be in a line like ducks. A good project might have been crosswalks. The refugees were searching for a quiet spot to die. In this sense they were reverting to the animal, to the atavistic dog inside all of us. Crawling to the other side reminded me of Joey. He was a slightly crazy old man I used to drink with in Tucson. One night he got stabbed in the Esquire Club. He made it out the side door near the bathrooms where the whores and transvestites gave blow jobs and crawled across the street to the Manhattan. He just made it to the bar inside where he pulled himself up and then collapsed on the floor. He apparently was trying to order a drink and I guess he was dead pretty quick after he fell. People said that he was too good to die in the Esquire Club. He didn't like the way they poured. I never saw it that way. Both bars seemed the same to me, although history has a way of soaking into stools and upholstery. I guess I was blind to the outrages that had come before in the Esquire Club, things that Joey knew about. As I drove along the road and watched the people crawl, I figured Joey would understand everything I was seeing since the whole thing was a disgrace, such a goddamned outrage on the other side of the road.

PANAMA

THE BRIGADIER GENERAL
AND ALL THAT IS GOLDEN

I WAS STANDING in the brigadier general's sunroom on a quiet, wide street in Quarry Heights during the final years of the U.S. military occupation of the Panama Canal Zone. There was a party and the general staff were all there.

My time in Rwanda was still fresh in my mind. I'd seen way too many dead people. My wife and son were in the living room playing with the general's golden retriever, and a junior officer itching to kill someone asked me about the dead, how there were so many of them in Africa, and did I have trouble sleeping?

I told him it wasn't the dead that bothered me, it was the dying. The dead lay silent in my dreams like soft, mossy logs in a rag-ridden forest waiting to melt into the earth. The dead were ready to feed a plant or a bug, to be tossed onto a fire, or dropped into a deep hole. After a while they become part of the landscape, something to be contemplated and easy to pitch a tent upon.

The dying were different, they tried to grab your legs as you staggered around or kicked at you if you stepped on them or called to you in that strange language that we haven't learned yet. They vomited on your shoes or scratched your arms or fell at your feet and begged for something without name.

They had a way of capturing your eyes, trying to pull you into their misery, into the dark holes that cradled them. They formed a barrier around your psyche and did everything in their power to keep you awake.

The dying never gave up and they stayed with you for as long as you lived, for as long as you were able to remember.

I told the soldier that with any luck all of us would be in Bosnia soon and he could see for himself if what I was saying was bullshit or not.

I walked into the room where my son was playing with the general's beautiful dog and the sunset was transforming the space into my own personal refuge. The light wove the words I had just spoken into a golden skin that I wore for the rest of the party.

No one could see me as long as I kept the skin on, but later that night I took it off and made love with my wife and then when everyone in Panama City was asleep I stole into my son's bedroom and stroked his golden hair goodnight.

I worried about him. How would he make his way through a failing world?

I wondered about leaving things behind as I watched the light of the dawn weave my thoughts into a new skin and when it was finished it hung suspended, quivering in the cool air and golden like all the rest.

I gazed at it for a moment and then slowly, painfully put it on.

It shone brightly and I knew it would be blinding.

My leather bag was usually stuffed with money. Cash was how to get things done in a war zone. We sent bundles of $10,000 and $20,000 into Somalia and the Sudan. In Bosnia, the normal shipment was $200,000. When the money went missing, there was no recourse. Stolen money was a low priority when compared to the fashions of war. One day a British ex-Royal Logistics Corps driver came in with a nasty cut under his eye and a story about how he went off the road and a group of Bosniaks robbed him. They got $220,000. He soon disappeared like a ghost from a Dickens' novel. Reporting the crime to the Bosnian and Croatian police was an unfunny joke. A few months later I got a visit from an ex-FBI agent, but he seemed more interested in finding good Italian food than the stolen money. I sent a letter to INTERPOL, but it was a bit outside their mandate. Then there was the time that $20,000 went missing on a Nairobi airline desk. A pretty receptionist was minding it. A driver was blamed, but I figured it was my old friend. He had a son going to the University of Edinburgh and that was expensive. In Rwanda and the Congo during the genocide I walked around with $25,000 in my bag. My traveling companion, who I was certain was CIA, would push me to buy expensive olives and cheese. Most of the money went for comic taxes, protection, inflated fuel, and high-priced compound rents. In other words, it was stolen legally. There were safes cracked and staff robbed at gunpoint and a few offices blown up. I got to where I hated cash money. It looked like the *omens of my bad decisions. Of course, the cash stolen in Iraq and Afghanistan ran into the billions. That money was in fresh $100 bills. I guess I should feel insulted. Most of the money stolen under my unique direction was dirty local currency that somebody had to pile into the back of a truck like plastic sacks of recyclable trash. When I went to my donor contacts about the robberies, they said they didn't want to hear about them. They had other things to worry about like genocide, poison gas and dirty bombs; but what really kept them up at night were the upcoming visits from their bosses in Washington and New York. Stolen money, as one guy told me, was a single line item lost in a mile high budget of massive waste. War, he went on, had a way of eating money and stolen money was a mere burp.*

ZIMBABWE

ALONA AND THE SCENTED GARDEN

WE WERE EATING a real Danish meal. There was smoked fish, pork, butter, cheese, strawberry jam, wine, beer, wafers, rye bread, olives, and cut vegetables. My face was red and rising from a reaction to Durban Poison. I was at the house of my expat boss from the Ministry of Home Affairs.

As we spread the pate, I made a proposal to the father, the mother, and their young daughter. "Look, since Alona is only fourteen years old, I obviously can't ask her to marry me. This ain't India, but in four years she'll be eighteen and I'll be thirty-four, only sixteen years difference."

The father frowned, but the mother seemed interested and Alona smiled at me. The girl and I had become great pals. She was fourteen going on twenty and she carried herself as if on the verge of spilling out into an unfathomable woman that could drown just about any man who got to near her edge.

I'd read some of her poetry. For a kid, it was pretty devastating. Nothing much had happened to her, but she wrote like she had sat against a shadowed wall watching people do bad things. The poetry was complimented by her impressionistic paintings that were worthy of a high-priced psychoanalyst. Perhaps her imagination was too dark for her innocent sensibilities.

She had mentioned to me that the storms coming up from the plains of South Africa were full of strange scents that had affected her mind. That maybe the movement of lions and the struggle of the Zulu had gotten into her blood. The inquietude had led her to weeping quietly on the corners of her bed.

The whole falling down thing was in her eyes. They were dark green with yellow specks. In many ways they were frightening. I understood her glances and gazes to be youthful prodigy and all four of us knew that she was different, not totally of this world.

Her IQ was around 150 and she spoke four languages with black humor and the twist of a young girl's knife. The extra dividend was her Scandinavian beauty supported by long gamine legs, straight blonde hair, and white marble skin that had faint purple blood lines in the hands. A young, attractive, intelligent, and mysterious girl: a killer combination in more ways than one.

I looked at her and she said with full lips, "I like the idea. I mean, I do, forever."

We all laughed, even the father.

I continued: "I'd write her every month and in four years if she has met someone else, then that would be fine. But if not, I'd ask for her hand and if she accepted, then we could marry and you two would become my parents. I'd get to call you mom and dad. What do you say?" The father said, "I don't think so," but the mother said, "Well why not?"

The mother was three years older than me; slightly more beautiful than her daughter and a bit harder, with less spontaneity.

"I can think of plenty of reasons," said the father, who was six years my senior. We all had another laugh.

On my last day in Harare I came to say goodbye to Alona. We sat on the veranda of her home; the sunlight broken in the trees. Our conversation moved along the falls of her sad song, each note dropping us to the next ledge. She wanted to control her own life, to infuse all things with the power that resided in her emerging heart. Her words had a certain deep color and I rested inside of them, looking through their transparent walls upon a world waiting to pounce.

"We can be together," she said. I was an image in one of her poems. "In the future...I'll be different and ready for you." Her green eyes glistened and a tear verged in the corner and neither one of us could hear the noise outside her compound walls.

We hung onto the moment and a chapter of our made-up story closed and then she reached her hand and picked a piece of lint off my shirt. She looked at me and I took her hand from my chest and we walked to the gate.

Of course, none of it ever happened. The whole notion was too odd, even for me. There were other things I needed to do; secret messages to decode. They were like whispers in the next room that I couldn't quite hear. Anyway, I wasn't the marrying kind; not even under those mildly pedophilic circumstances which had a sort of weak magnetic attraction pulling along the swirling electrons of men and women from 10,000 years ago.

The mother wrote me three years later, one year before our wedding might have taken place.

Alona had become depressed and tried to kill herself in a Swiss boarding school. The mother said no one understood her daughter at the school. She and her husband had placed trust in the administrators. The school had such a great reputation. When the father was appointed to a high position in the European Union everything moved too fast. They were distracted. Only a day at the school to get Alona into a room and then they were off to Brussels.

The prose in her letter was disturbing and she had adopted a stream of consciousness style that unlocked the dark closets of her mind and let me briefly enter into the spaces where she kept her shoes and sex toys. I understood very well and it seemed as if she was going insane.

At the end of her letter she wrote, "Alona is such a unique girl. You know, I was hoping your proposal was real. We could have had such fun together. It would have been so strange, so wonderful to do something like that. We could have lain together in our scented garden."

In quiet moments I wonder about taking Alona for my bride. Sometimes I imagine myself standing in the scented garden, but on a winter's day. I can see the scene clearly in my mind.

The white cloud of my breath and the saturated sky are my only companions. I am like an ice statue from another planet looking with frozen eyes through a window at Alona. She turns a book page before an unfettered fire and her movements are smooth and beautiful. The sound of her youth chases me down the short hall of mortality and I can't keep up. There is the fantasy of youth and the reality of a passing year. Our minds and dreams are awash in make-believe, but our bodies are always counting the moments as we hesitate and stagger.

I suppose I could have followed up with the proposal and attempted love beneath the phases of our shared moon; watching the orb during the day, waiting in our bed for its message at night. Overall though, I'm happy I didn't marry the fourteen-year-old. I really didn't want to know the origin of her sad looks. The glow of the mother would probably have been injurious and eventually the candy and flowers on my shelves would have turned stale and dry, so near to the ideal of Alona.

You can't go down that road. It's too dangerous. They shot a soldier off a truck in the food convoy yesterday. The bullet didn't kill him. He broke his neck when he fell into a ditch. Well, so who shot him? We don't know, but somebody did. They always shoot the guy with the gun I thought. So we left that night and drove down the road through all the child soldier checkpoints and past the burned out trucks and finally we had to leave the road at a fallen bridge. Napoleon sat with his engine idling and offered me some khat. We chewed for a few minutes and then crashed through the bush with our lights cutting the darkness like a soldier on a horse slashing the enemy with his sword and we gripped anything we could as we rode on. We expected to fall into a hole, but we didn't. When we finally got to the Red Cross hospital with our three sick women and one kid, the guard at the gate asked where we were coming from. When we answered, he said the road was too dangerous for travel. I told him that sometimes it is hard to tell exactly how dangerous roads are unless you go down them. Had something happened to us, then we would have confirmed the road was dangerous. Getting through without a scratch raised a little doubt about the level of risk. Except for those who said, well he's just a damn fool and lucky to boot, because that road's dangerous; putting those refugees at risk, what an idiot.

HONDURAS

STANLEY LOVES HUMPHREY BOGART

WITHOUT MUCH WARNING our outboard lost compression. Stanley worked on it for a while and then gave up. We looked at each other. Without a motor we couldn't get through. We were in a very tight passageway clogged with high swamp grass that protected mutants from the outside world. Evil looking creatures hung around in the infected trees. I started having an attack of pre-stings and pre-bites.

Our paddle was next to useless. The water of Brus Lagoon suddenly withdrew its invitation and in a pique asked when and how we might be going home? There was nothing but green and yellow savannah as far as you could see which in our case was about six feet.

The only option was to drag the boat through the rivulets and muddy grass and get back to a decent waterway. Neither of us thought much of that since we were pretty deep into the lagoon. Stanley asked if I had ever seen "The African Queen." I was stunned. Stanley was a Mosquito Indian who had lived in La Mosquitia all his life.

"Sure, but where did you see it?"

"In San Pedro whorehouse, on video at bar. Good movie. That man was drunk. Big drunk."

Stanley was a critic of drunks. He didn't like falseness in the act of drinking. There was only one reason to drink and that was to get so drunk you passed out or got into a fight and somebody knocked you out. Inauthentic drinking was a violation, like saving money or keeping a promise to an asshole.

The existentialists had nothing on Stanley.

"Drunk named Allnut. Remember?"

"Allnut? Are you sure?" I asked.

"Yep," he replied as he turned around and dug through his bag. He found a fifth of rum and a big jar of locally brewed Indian poison. "Let's do what that guy Allnut did."

So we spent a few minutes drinking until we didn't mind jumping into the water and pulling the boat through the lagoon. We killed snakes and scared the wildlife along the way. Slimy, scaly things moved across our skin and bit at our fingers.

We started off laughing and then changed pretty quickly to cussing. Sometimes we felt smart and carried and pushed the boat across mud flats to other shallow spots that seemed to afford more water and fewer weeds.

That night we stopped and lay in the boat. We were exhausted and drank the last of our alcohol. The Bug Lords of Earth called upon us. Each clap of our hands killed ten or so mosquitoes. We only took a swig when we estimated there were more than two or three hundred buzzing around us.

Mosquitoes in our mouths counted double. Anything less and we waited.

We talked about Humphrey Bogart. Stanley was interested in how movies were made. I told him the basics. He wanted to know about the acting part, so I described the camera and sets and how you learned your lines and how money fell down from the sky on top of your head and beautiful women hid in your bed waiting for you to come home.

"I can do that," said Stanley.

We kept talking and spent a sleepless night like a two-headed Allnut. We were interrupted by a tapir being killed somewhere in the darkness. A leopard or crocodile had this one and the scream was disturbing for all of us, particularly the tapir. We listened together and then everything got quiet.

Dying tapirs are like telescopes taking a bead on our old fears, our ancient past, and when they are no more, we won't be too far behind.

At first light we continued our struggle. Finally we found the stream that had brought us in and we paddled until we got back to the Patuca. We said goodbye to the caimans and hoary turtles and from there it was an easy drift down to Barra Patuca and the ex-slave pirates we employed.

Nobody believed us when we told our story. The prospectors, whores and traders laughed at us. They said nobody could carry a boat out of Brus Lagoon, we were full of shit.

Stanley sat contemplating the insults for a few seconds, then bolted straight up, sending people scrabbling as he howled like a wild dog. He threw his beer bottle against the wall. He had the scene down perfectly.

When he was like that he always ended up threatening to kill somebody, but then he'd collapse unconscious into two millennium of Indian history. The other drunks turned away and laughed at something else. The show was over as Stanley lay there in a restful, heavy-breathing heap. It was a beautiful thing to watch, like a movie.

In this respect, he was adding a new dimension to the character of Charlie Allnut from the "African Queen", as if someone had come up with a script to show how the booze had finally defeated Allnut in his later years, how the tertiary syphilis he had acquired along the Congo River had finally turned his brain into a chunk of moldy cheese.

It's too bad Stanley never made it to Hollywood. He could have been big.

She threw herself down at my feet. A few weeks ago I had given her a chance to be my cook. I'd seen her building a little cardboard and plastic shack against the outer wall of my compound. She was pretty and looked reasonable. A driver told me she was a widow. Although nearly every cook in the country was a man, I thought maybe I should give a destitute woman a chance. Now she was crying, kissing my flip flops. My office manager stood there frowning and shaking his head. He bent over and reached for her, but she grabbed my legs and hung on. The problem was she had started flirting with me and at lunch she had pressed her breasts into my ears while I was trying to eat the cucumbers and rice she was serving. I couldn't have my Islamic staff thinking I was having sex with the cook, so I had been forced to let her go. The problem was timing. Had I been younger and without position, I would not have minded moving into her lean-to on the street and sleeping with her for weeks or as long as I could take it, but that was impossible now, unless I was willing to give up the big house and the big job and the small salary for a pretty widow and a brick wall to lean against. I had already done things like that. Timing, it's all about timing, I kept saying, but I don't think she could hear me. She was screaming in a high pitched voice. My dog answered in a forlorn howl. Over the next few weeks I would look down and there she would be looking up at me with a mix of hatred and disappointment in her eyes and then one day she was gone. Another woman moved into the shed. She was definitely a bad cook. I could tell just by looking at her since she was more beautiful than my old female cook had ever thought of being.

THAILAND

A VERY SMALL MOMENT

I OPENED MY EYES, but there was nothing to see, not even the mosquito net. Night had created another type of black, something for criminals. I held my missing hand in front of my eyes and moved it down to touch my nose. Was I buried inside a coffin? Maybe I was dead, except I was still thinking, still breathing. I tried to visualize what I looked like, but I couldn't make it out. My mind was heavy, filled with noteworthy water, as I waited for the camp to come alive. It was about 3:00 a.m.

I drifted in and out of consciousness. The web of my yearning strung around me and movement was dense in a ragged dream. A sticky substance pulled me down and then a remote light came on somewhere down a long hall. Basil came through the dark like atomic particles. I could barely make him out. I called to him, but he was unable to hear. His plastic, opium-bent body was underneath a naked light bulb and he had a white, worn tone.

He was reading a letter from his wife who was terminally ambivalent toward him. His children missed him desperately. He loved his kids. They only knew him as pop and not as a sketchy doctor battered by a high profile malpractice suit. Mum had kept that from them.

I fully awoke with a moan on my bamboo bed. The ghost of Basil vanished. My feet moved around looking for flip flops and a flashlight. I decided to check out the opium ward down the path, maybe drink an iced soda. Movement inside the doctor's office caught my eye. As I walked past open windows, I saw shadows against the wall. Basil was making coffee in the glow of a few candles.

I poked my head in the door. "Good evening Doctor," I said. "Any good bets on the floor?"

Basil frowned. I smiled and continued, "Night shift, you know, we could do hours, a long shot if you want. But only if there's something serious."

It was all about the big wheel, as if we knew anything about that. We often passed the time by betting on the condition of refugees in the hospital. Sometimes we'd bet on patients dying within hours, sometimes weeks. Short-term dying usually went with good money odds. 5 to 1 were typical on a quick death. I'd look for addicts on the opium ward with complications, like respiratory failure or diseased organs or, the jackpot, sudden death without any identifiable cause. I'd hit a few sudden deaths.

Basil had been controlling his opium use for about five years. Unless you knew his habits, he seemed normal. As he sometimes said, "The problem is not the dope; it is the lack of dope." Fortunately, this was the Golden Triangle, so a pure, cheap source was not a problem. Still, he was too thin and very fragile, like a Japanese porcelain doll balancing on the edge of a high shelf.

He turned to me and said, "You bugger. Want to make up for the last one, do you?"

He had won our most recent bet. It had been an old lowland Lao addict who had stumbled into the hospital on sticks. Breathing had not been his thing. He looked like a dried noodle. I'd taken the old guy to die within five days. Not only did he not die, but Basil turned him into a recognizable human being with arms, legs, and a face.

The old man walked out of the opium ward under his own power and had gotten on a bus. Basil had bought him an all-expense paid trip to the Vientiane bridge with the even money I'd lost, 500 Baht.

"That'll teach you to fuck with me, my wee laddie."

I searched the opium ward. The cat was asleep. The hospital sang all the old tunes. The refugees were stealing the air from the locals. One of the good looking Thai nurses was dozing on a cot. Nearly all the beds were taken.

Refugees liked opium, but now were paying the price by complaining, cramping, vomiting, pulling against the ropes that tied them down, and generally acting like they were dying and in some cases they were.

The addicts were mostly young, and here and there an expat who wanted to kick. Foreigners came up from Bangkok on a trek and then got strung out. The elderly refugees hardly ever bothered to check themselves into the place; they generally looked upon opium as a free pass to help them enter the spirit world of their ancestors without too much pain.

A young woman with a little boy about two years old caught my eye. I stood on a stain of vomit and blood, watching the little fellow's head rolling from side to side. He wore a skull cap with small metal dangle balls and bells. They clinked as his head flopped around. His breathing was irregular and his face looked like an unhappy map of my future.

One of the H'Mong orderlies walked by and I asked what was going on with the mother and child. He told me she was an addict and the kid had "unresponsive to standard treatment malaria" or as the orderly said, "He bad with bad kind."

Bingo, the little boy was a winner, two days, maximum. Basil would go for that. He wanted the hopeless cases, particularly children. I'd try to double up on my last bet, get two to one on 500 Baht.

Basil had to keep him alive for 48 hours; otherwise I'd win 1,000 Baht. "If anyone can do it, it's me," said Basil, without a smile.

I left the hospital and decided to visit the grandfather of my interpreter. His hut was at the top of the rim and it had a view across the valley where 15,000 H'Mong were encamped.

Their world was the border and the war with the Pathet Lao. Old men would cry and tell me stories of dead American friends. The H'Mong were charming people and they let me smoke their opium. My interpreter's grandfather was a solid, blue collar pipe mixer. He had arthritis and a goiter on his neck the size of a blimp over the Super Bowl.

The opium did wonders for him. I would lay with his dogs and old friends with health issues and we would all slow breathe our way into the remote thoughts that opium drew like a warm bath.

I wasn't an addict yet, but I did enjoy the recreational use of the drug.

Lying on my side, I put my head upon the knees of the person beside me. There was a shortage of pillows. We were all in fetal positions along with the unborn and the dying. Around in a circle we went.

The old man took his tray and worked a bit of opium into a soft ball. The fire light danced in the hut and the dogs snored and the old man moved in a way totally approved by the small, scattered French administration from eighty odd years ago. They had brought opium to the upcountry as a cash crop. The H'Mong eventually started to grow it and the old H'Mong who was now preparing my opium looked upon it as a medicine.

When you search for hypocrisy in the world, you need look no further than opium.

The tray held a candle in a small glass lamp and the pipe was ancient and we passed it from one to the other. After a few hits from the pipe, I drifted upon the shadows in the hut like a wooden boat floating down a slow moving river. My 1,000 Baht boy with malaria was on the bank. I watched as Basil put the big water needle in his belly for hydration.

The jungle was close when the moon waned and the breeze died and then I stood right beside Basil and there was stillness in the boy's eyes and then he went limp. The heart of a fool skipped a beat. The mother hardly showed any expression as her son hung tightly to his death.

The smoothness is in all of us. Some are more aware of it than others. I can see it at night when I lay my head down and close my eyes and fall asleep. It is a reflecting surface. Not exactly water, more like light hitting the imperfections of old world glass. It is deep in our brains and we watch, feeling the warmth of burning across a strange, ephemeral surface.

A small piece of me, somewhere deep in my brain, smoothed out onto the glowing screen as I lay there smoking opium. The color changed and it cast a primordial, distant light over my visions. The subdued brightness made me sweat in yellows and reds and flickers and dogs and a little kid dying in the arms of Basil down in the opium ward. All squeezed into a very small moment.

After a few hours I turned the pipe down and started to notice the hut. I managed to get to my feet and staggered outside into the dawn's mist. I fell once on my way to the hospital. When I got to the office I found Basil. His eyeballs had dropped into a cup of coffee. They bobbed for a moment and then disappeared. Without eyes he didn't look so well.

He told me how the little H'Mong child had died, and then he took his bag down from the wall, reached inside and came out with two dirty 500 Baht notes. I was a winner.

Basil was a sucker for these types of bets. His malpractice suit had involved the death of three little girls under his care and he was always trying to make up for the past. Reading your opponent in a game of chance is critical to a winning outcome.

I stuffed the money into my pocket and headed across the road to the bamboo hut I called home.

The old woman who ran the store nearby laughed at me as I stumbled alone. I slept all of that day and when I awoke to a slivered moon, I began to think about all that I was doing wrong. Betting on sick refugees was pretty close to the top of the list.

When you make bets on the dying they own you, perhaps for all time. There is something dangerous about the whole enterprise, particularly if you win money on their death. Over time they take possession of your mind and body. The strength of ownership depends upon your condition at any given moment. That was a key rule if one played the game and there was ruin there like free falling into an endless grave.

I decided to walk up the hill to the home of the old H'Mong who fixed the gummy pipe. Most of the refugees were in their huts and cardboard boxes eating the short rations the Thai afforded them. They were laughing and sat around fires waiting to return to Laos. Occasionally I'd smell opium in the air as I climbed up the hill.

I wasn't an addict, but I was a man trying to get away from himself, without moving. Opium was like that and I soon found myself on a small island populated by monsters. We all lived together fearing the crusade of the sea as it cut and diminished the ground beneath our feet.

There was one spot where they were sick and dying and they didn't need to be that way. The problem was getting food to them. I wanted a boat that could clear the shallows of the lagoon up into the small bay where the camp was located. The perfect boat was on an island just off the coast. A Finn and the director had brought it down from New Orleans. It was an oil supply boat with practically no draft and it was just sitting there. I had been told the Honduran authorities wouldn't issue the proper paperwork and because of that the U.N. refused to load food on it. When Pete and I went out, we found the captain screwing a whore and his men drinking along a rotting dock beside the boat. I immediately liked all of them. We partied for a few days together on the strange island built out of wood walkways drilled into reefs. We eventually made a night crossing to La Ceiba. We bribed the Harbor Master and got the necessary legal documents. By the next day the boat was fully loaded with food that I had taken from a U.N. warehouse without permission. As I watched the boat motor out of the harbor it listed heavily to the port side. A storm came that night and the boat almost sank. A passenger on board pulled a gun and demanded a lifeboat. The captain had to brain him with a club. When they got close enough to shore they threw him overboard in a life vest. The boat began to supply the little camp of refugees on a regular basis and their health improved. Getting that boat up and running broke all the rules. I was very proud of the whole thing. Whoring, drinking to excess, bribing officials, forging manifests, a near disaster at sea, and fully supporting my captain when he tossed some idiot with a gun overboard; taken together, it did the trick. I was working for a Christian agency. They knew all about me and prayed for my soul. I guess they tolerated my ways because they were Christians. I was going to hell; that much was certain. I will probably find some of those same Christians in hell. Most of them seemed like hypocrites. In general, I think it is easier to get to hell if one is a fraud waving the Bible around than if you are an expedient atheist like me. Anyway, I am looking forward to going so I can see who is there. My days are now down to the smaller numbers so it shouldn't be too much longer.

HONDURAS

THE MAN WHO COULDN'T COME

THE RIVER WAS ABOVE the natural markers he used to gauge depth and danger. An overnight storm had brought it up and he had never seen the water so high. The sun was shining as he swung gently in the hammock on his porch. Little gold sparks danced upon the river's strong current as his mind drifted. Up in the mountains faint thunder sounded and he imagined the river would continue to rise through the day.

His house was last in a line of tents and wood structures that stretched along the river and stopped just short of the thick vegetation and towering trees. He was on a little hill and had a good view of the river about fifty meters away. The heavy rain had created white water where normally massive boulders could be seen. Birds and butterflies were everywhere and the humidity and dampness were fierce. He enjoyed the peaceful seclusion.

Normally he would have been at work by now, but there was a food distribution up in the camp and he really didn't have much to do; the U.N. was in charge. The main point of his work was to create traditional barter markets for the refugee Mosquito Indians. They needed a place to sell their crops.

The Contras had been drawn to the project, looking for money, equipment, and food. He was finding war politics in the jungle interesting, but after walking to isolated villages over the last few days, he was tired. A little time off sounded good, he'd take the opportunity to read a book or write a letter in solitude.

Thankfully the breeze stirred up from the water and passed over his body. He was naked except for a pair of frayed cutoffs. He lightly moved his hand over his sensitive left nipple and felt the warm tingle.

Women who he had known sexually came to mind. He started counting them, but decided he needed a pencil and paper. He couldn't keep the number and order straight. A few of the memories were in the haze of alcohol and pot, but yet he could see them. Sometimes he thought that maybe he was addicted to women, to what they did for him.

He dropped the idea of listing all the women and settled on calculating the different nationalities of his lovers. That was easier to hold. One mental tally mark for each country, even though he might have had more than one woman from the same place. He visualized a global map and the blue oceans. Sex on airplanes and ships were given special dispensation. He rejected chronological order.

Pretty faces and nude bodies appeared and he flew over the landscapes and entered dark rooms: Mexico, the United States, El Salvador, Guatemala, Honduras, Panama, Nicaragua, Thailand, Laos, Cambodia, Bangladesh, Austria, France, Germany, Spain, Italy, Belgium, England, Ireland, Lesotho, KwaZulu, Transkei, South Africa, and finally two ships and a plane. A few he had paid for, most not. That was all he could remember.

He wondered if it was fair to count the horror of apartheid and the artificial "countries" of KwaZulu and Transkei. He remembered the Zulu and the Xhosa girls and watched himself with them.

The Zulu lived in a cave above the town of Maseru. She kept a monkey and cats. They built fires during snowstorms and drank at the hotel bars. Her name was Mary and when they blew the candles out and made love, he couldn't see her as he dived into her buttery skin. She had named him "funny mzungu with soft hands" and she failed to teach him how to be expertly rough like the Zulu men from the mines.

The Xhosa had been interesting. Their time together was brief. He had met her while trekking and she had smeared white mud on his naked body in the shadows of her small hut and passed a flower with her tongue into his mouth that brought mutual hallucinations.

He finally decided that it would be permissible to count the apartheid homelands.

As he wandered over the world remembering different women, he thought if people knew about the list they would probably call him disgusting or boastful or lucky. However he was judged, the list represented his feelings about marriage and monogamy. The first was an artifice designed to perpetuate the power of church and state, while the second was genetically abnormal for humans.

The surprising thing about his sexual past was that he rarely had orgasms with his partners. Of the many times he had had sex, climaxes were very rare and unforgettable. The remembrance of orgasms had to substitute for the real thing and he kept them on display like trophies in a glass case.

Before he made love to women he always asked two questions: were they free of STDs and did they take birth control. If they said yes to both, he would reply that he too was healthy and by the way, they should not expect him to come. The second statement always brought a quizzical look and smile to their faces. They never believed him.

His lack of orgasms often led to ill will from his partners. Women would go dry in the effort and although he always warned them about long encounters and parched interiors, they never understood until it occurred.

After an hour or so of copulation, discomfort normally set in and eventually the women would either fake or actually have a final orgasm. Afterward, they became desperate to please him. They would say things like, "Don't worry, you'll come with me," or "I can do what you want," or "Let's try this." Still the results were questionable.

It was in these moments that he realized that women had a kind of sexual pride different from men. Mutual pleasure for most women was one of the keys to their being. Even if they were selfish, they still had strong self-pride in their attractiveness and ability to please men. When the softness of their bodies failed to deliver, inadequacy and recrimination settled upon the bed.

Some accused him of being gay or abused or manipulative or maybe diseased. He denied the conditions, the pathologies. As they lay resting, he would tell them why he thought he couldn't come.

It had to do with the fear of bringing life into the world without preparation and agreement. As a young boy he had struggled with medical problems. Sometimes he couldn't breathe. Hospital bills had brought financial stress to his family and as he grew older, he felt guilty. His birth had been unplanned.

The projection of his past fell upon sexual encounters. Self was more important than society. When he felt the fluid rising up his penis, something inside of him cut it off and forced it back down into the testicles. The process was familiar and automatic during acts of congress, even oral and manual.

He could always tell when a woman wanted to have a baby with him. In moments of extreme excitement, their legs tried to detain him. He could see the expectation of progeny in their eyes. Chemicals were set off inside his brain that alerted his penis to the ancient trap of unwanted responsibilities.

He had only made one mistake; there was an abortion in his past. One night while loud music played, he had intensely climaxed. They were both surprised. Relaxation and contentment descended upon them, and then a month later the pregnancy became known.

"Are you sure," she said with a distant look.

"It would ruin all of our plans. We're not married, we don't have jobs, nothing in the bank," he almost begged. She kept tapping her fingers on the table as she smoked a cigarette. Her body was like a major river delta, fertile beyond imagination. This would be her fourth abortion if they continued and, in the end, they did.

The nurse brought the plastic bucket onto the long balcony where he waited. He watched the sloshing of fluid and form as she approached.

She was going to the outside stairway that led to the medical waste incinerator in the basement. As she passed him she spit out that he was the father of a boy. Her words were sharp, hurtful and he imagined the little heart of his son burning in the fire. The memory of the abortion had been partitioned off into a little locked box and he had tried to lose the key.

The sound of fingernails scratching across a wood board drew him back. He looked down the porch and saw a Mosquito girl sitting on the steps. She was about 20 years old and her back was to him and he noticed she wore a white crop top and a heavy denim skirt. He could see the tops of her hips just below her waist line. She had long, straight black hair and it shone in the morning light.

She turned and smiled at him. Her lips were red. He returned the smile and in Spanish he asked her what she wanted. She giggled and said she had seen him bathing in the river the day before and wanted to meet him.

Her family was up in the camp and she had come from Nicaragua only three days ago. Although she lived in Puerto Cabezas, she had been visiting the WaWa region when the Contras forced everyone in her home village across the border. She smiled as she said, "I am a refugee."

Many years ago he had made the decision never to have sex with refugees or the displaced. The ban did not extend to local populations, but target groups were off limits, even the whores, maybe mostly the whores.

She looked at him for a moment and then said for 20 Lempira she would go into his room. Her brother was nearby on the path and she would call him and give him the money and he would go to the store and buy some good food for their meal that night.

He told her there was plenty of food up at the U.N. distribution and to get off his porch and not come back. When she rose he could see her fine figure. She was definitely a professional and hard in the way of some Mosquito Indian girls.

As she walked away, he got out of the hammock and went into his room. He shared it with a Honduran engineer, but the roommate would not return until late in the day. He decided to masturbate. He imagined the Indian girl and within a few minutes was finished.

He cleaned himself and walked over to the window and looked down on the rising river. The girl from his porch was bathing with her top off and her full breasts looked very beautiful. Her denim skirt was still on. The brother, had there really been one, was gone. He thought about how she could have been in his room and then she waded out further. She leaned forward, tottering and suddenly the rain fed current took her. He watched as she bobbed and splashed in the middle of the river and within a few seconds she was under the surface of the white water, heading into the jungle, on her way down to the sea.

Sometimes the ghosts come to me. Not much to do, but watch: I'm running as fast as I can. Come on Come On. They can't be far behind. Who's the fastest runner? No question they are, but we are running for our lives. My big feet are bleeding and the villages are destroyed. Got to keep going, the sun's down, but can't stop. The moon will do. They're going to kill us. They're naked with AK-47s and they fire them wildly, but that doesn't mean they can't kill us. Is this how I have to be to be who I am? Come on Come On, run with me now. We can make it. But I didn't make it and neither did my baby nor Come On, my dog. They are gone now and my husband has married more white women and killed more people and is a vice president and everything is like the things you read in books and the newspapers and in movie scripts. I didn't think about those things back then. Everything was too alive and real and then it all ended inside my Volkswagen. But you know, I never doubted anything, I couldn't. I was falling too fast to see the blurred images passing away from me. Love and death came over me too quickly, but I guess that was how it had to be. I was leading a life filled with star dust and every night it poured into my heart as I lay inside my earthen room. I could never get enough of my personal stars above the Sudan and now they will fill me forever. The ghosts finally fade away and I think about them; watch them as they dissolve into the shadows on my wall, and then I roll over and clear my mind. I can hear Teresa breathing and slowly I fall asleep and dream about running with dogs.

BANGLADESH

THE LEPER COLONY

A HAWK HUNTS high overhead. The white shiny rooftop of my SUV reflects in his eyes as my arm hangs out the window. Had I been a real rat, instead of a human facsimile, I am sure the bird would have had more interest in my dangling flesh. My vehicle makes poor time in the wind as I let my mind wander away from my destination and the nastiness I expect.

I have been depressed for a few years now. Maybe my personality is shallow or maybe there have been too many women, too many dead babies. Who knows? Some say I'm a bastard, others that I'm an asshole, and between the two I prefer being a bastard. The other is too pedestrian for my tastes.

My despair, phony or not, has led me to think about drowning myself in the endless Brahmaputra, the son of the Brahma. The thought is just developing, but the images are calm and cool.

If you have to sink in a river, this is the one. The ugly words in my mouth should take me down pretty quickly. I've been storing the really vile ones in the cavities of my teeth. It's cheaper than going to the dentist and a lot less painful, at least in the short run.

I visualize my head going under and then feel the pull of the current as I swirl toward the Bay of Bengal and the massive Indian Ocean beyond.

Since this is Bangladesh, there are many others in the water with me. Our silhouettes slowly revolve as we wave unseen to those on shore.

We extend our arms in that lazy, uncaring way of the dead and with the help of fish and thin cloth we form a little community of entwined spirits. We shape schools and markets and go to work and float along and never have to die again. Food is worthless. The taxing authorities are helpless and nobody goes to jail.

The riverbed slowly avoids our time, but we are unaware.

I do have a few friends, but they are just as troubled as I am. My poor decisions have caused the helpless to die and because of that, I drink too much, have winged with an array of drugs, and said mean, unfortunate things to people who thought they knew me. I have been particularly unkind to women, even those who have sincerely tried to help me.

Commitment is impossible for me, so I have lied to have sex or paid for it. Nothing unusual about that, except that for non-whores my flakiness comes as a very big surprise. I guess it is the misreading of my character that causes ex-lovers to become angry.

I have been engaged seven times, but some of those were not very serious and only a few involved rings. I have paid for three abortions and left two women on the altar. They were sisters and the canceled ceremonies were separated by two years and a lot of deception. A friend of the women put a contract on me with some of his low-life associates from across the border. "Don't kill him, but give the bastard something to look at for the rest of his miserable life."

They found me and I have trouble picking up tiny things.

I know none of this is right, but whoever said love, sex, responsibility, independence, and death have to be uniform across human stories? That sounds boring. I equate love with death, sex is like fuel, responsibility is a lion chasing me, and independence is the air I breathe. The kicker is I am continually redefining all of these words in my mind. I have little success in explaining who I am to people.

Emptiness has become more than a bottle and I am starting to worry about the lies and the ridicule. The existential dog that has been chasing me is now within barking distance.

I stop strangling myself, because exactly at that moment we pull into one of the older police stations in the district of Mymensingh. I have been summoned by an urgent phone call.

The place was built during the times of the British East India Company and I half expect to find a 200-year old Brit in a pith helmet inside, but instead, a scowling policeman leads me to a cell where I find one of my drivers lying in a pool of piss and vomit. He is one of the few Hindus on my staff.

Our eyes meet and I see that his two front teeth have been sheared in half. He is sobbing as he describes how the police beat him and tossed him head first onto the concrete floor for no reason other than he was driving a new Toyota SUV and a local judge wanted to take it for a spin.

After paying a fine, sweet talking the judge, arguing with the cops, recovering the vehicle, and stretching the released driver in the back seat, we all head home in a sullen funk.

I roll the window down and let the night wind blow my hair. I feel like a great administrator cut out of the same white cloth that wrought the British Empire. The full moon thinks those kind of thoughts are funny. "You're no Brit," she whispers, "and what's more, I'm going to tell Bonga, the sun god, that you are a stuffed man." The monsoon clouds chuckle.

I find comfort in the likelihood that few people can hear weather systems bitch. No one in the SUV seems to be listening. So I say under my breath that I know all about Bonga. "I've been on the sun's bad side more than once and I really don't care," I bluster.

It is not hard to imagine that you are part of the British Raj in this country. The old limey ghost envelopes you wherever you go, whatever you do. There is the soggy block construction, the bad food, the little Connaught circles, the absurd bureaucracy, the insecure pride, and the clipped British accent that comes out of everyone's mouth.

The Indians, of course, morphed it all into their own independent nation; a horrifying two headed Hindu and Muslim dog with a British skeleton. Every so often it attempts to eat itself and one day it may be successful at the expense of the rest of us.

I don't hold anything against the British, the Pakistanis, the Indians, or the Bangladeshis. I am focused on something else.

Despite thoughts of suicide, I have decided to give romance or at least regular sex, one more chance. In my pocket is an invitation to visit the only decent looking female expatriate in this part of the country. She is an English volunteer nurse working at one of Father Damien's leper colonies and after a good night's sleep I intend to find out what she is all about.

She is apparently as desperate as I am, but evidently for different reasons. A happy little Catholic nun, who likes to tell risqué jokes, has set the whole thing up. She and the English volunteer work together in the colony. According to the nun, "the poor girl's social life revolves around the lepers. She needs something more, a chance to have a good time outside of what they want to do. Lepers can be so demanding."

When I first heard about her I had my doubts. Over the years I have noticed that English women can have strong teeth and sometimes wear saddles, but then the nun mentioned, "Oh, she was in a Guinness calendar."

My fears quickly changed into their party clothes.

The next morning I am up before dawn. I pack a shirt, flip flops, and a bottle of second-rate Czech absinthe chased into my bag by a pound sack of limes. I am going without a driver, since I am hoping to take advantage of the lonely girl and spend a few relaxing nights in her bed. The trip takes about 5 hours and stretches up into the tea country.

The road is mostly clear. I pass the time by feeling the push of a waning monsoon wind from the south. I am so intent upon keeping my vehicle on the road, hours go by like the names of old friends I can't recall. It is a bit scary when the road sign tells me I am there.

As I turn into the leper colony I see large open fields of gardens and grazing animals. The buildings are spotlessly white and look like barracks. The lower halves of the trees are painted white and white rocks edge everything else that can't get away.

I park my vehicle in front of what looks like the main building. There is a large sign that says, "Father Damien Welcomes You." As I get out a woman of perhaps 30-years or so comes down the steps. She has blonde hair and blue eyes that are shining a light on me. She walks in slow motion as my mind tries to comprehend what I am seeing. Hollywood movies are sprinkled with faces and bodies like hers. I immediately know I want to screw her. She extends her hand a good 20 feet from me and calls out, "You're here. Thanks for coming." I reach out and we touch.

Over the next several hours I learn about leprosy. If this is foreplay, it is new to me. I start to get the feeling this girl is a saint. We seem to be attracted to each other, but the lepers are always interfering when I try to steer the conversation in a different direction, one that might involve us kissing at some point.

As we walk across the quad I accidentally graze my hand across hers. She reacts well and steps off balance in front of me. Our bodies press together for a moment. I touch her shoulder and she stabilizes with a smile.

"The grass is dangerous," she laughs.

"The gardens look beautiful. Can you show them to me?"
At that moment a leper crawls out from behind a shrub almost tripping me for real. "Ranadip," she chortles. "Let me introduce you to our pride and joy. This is our macramé champion, Sir Ranadip."
Sir Ranadip is an amazing mess. His nose and ears are gone. He crawls and hops like some sort of monkey bird as we move along the field. "Come," he says. "Let's do pot holders today! Yes, pot holders would be good, very good!"
I listen to the leper shout with joy despite his deteriorating body. The beautiful English nurse is like the Times Square of his life and apparently every day is New Year's Eve. I am swept along in a growing crowd. Other lepers come out of the shadows and by the time we get to Ranadip's room, I recall that I really, really hate macramé.
"Well, here we are," she says. "Do you want to join us?"
"Sure," I say with able bodied enthusiasm.
Everyone is laughing as they play with the string, beads, and rope. Ranadip uses his teeth and what is left of his toes and fingers to tie the knots. The others have more and longer extremities, but don't work nearly as well as Ranadip. I understand why he is the champion. There is art and magic to his motions.
My efforts are akin to a man trying to pick things up with bricks.
So through the day it is one thing after the other to help the lepers. I am all smiles. I wonder if the girl suspects anything. We eat with the nuns and then she finally takes me to her room. This is my big moment.
I pour us each a small glass of absinthe with a squeeze of lime. We sit in torn canvas camp chairs. She has an old rabbit eared T.V. that has an extended range due to a metal clothes hanger. We barely get a Dhaka station showing a silent Greta Garbo war movie. It is titled "Flesh and the Devil". Garbo ends up falling through a thin sheet of ice and dying, but not before she gives John Gilbert a blow-the-match-out cigarette kiss.
As my mind looks inward during the movie, I visualize a WWI trench and a soldier holding a carrier pigeon. He wraps a little slip of coded paper around the bird's leg. It is a message for the English girl. It says she should go to bed with me. Bombs are exploding and people are dying, but the pigeon, with those nervous pinpoint eyes and delicate neck flies up and away. With luck it will find the girl and she will get the message.

Believing I have built the proper foundation throughout a day of "helping out," I divine what I think is "the look" and catch her eyes just in that perfect moment. She surprises me and says, "I hope you don't mind sleeping in the ward. There's a cot just outside my door. Sometimes I sleep there. I don't think the patients will bother you."

"You mean the lepers who are sick?"

I guess just being a leper is not enough to get into the hospital. Something else needs to be wrong with them. "Not a problem at all," I say, but inside, tears fall for my dead pigeon.

My night is restless. I am depressed. I hear the lepers moving around, pulling on their sheets, going to the bathroom. There is a table at the far end of the ward lit by one of those portable gas lamps. Bugs buzz around it like the bi-planes in King Kong. A nun reads a book just inside the light. I drift in and out of sleep as the wind rattles the window above my head.

I awake tired. The wind is dead. Everything is dark on the floor. The lepers are sleeping and the holy nun is gone. The dawn slowly spreads in thin, almost invisible golden breaths across the large grass field just outside my window. I hear the short melody of a cuckoo bird.

I lift my head up and look out the window.

Ranadip sits in the center of the grass field. His ravaged body meditates in a perfect place and his eyes are closed. He wears a white loin cloth, nothing else. A small, spotted kid goat stands just beside him. Slowly the goat places his hooves on Ranadip's shoulders and then with a movement guided by Bonga, the kid goat jumps on his shoulders.

Life floods the parched regions of my heart. I am startled by the feeling.

The little goat is still for a split second and then he moves upward and places two hooves on Ranadip's head. With a final push toward the sky, the kid goat mounts the top of his head with all four hooves.

The pair are unmoving in time as the light of the sun caresses them and somewhere far away cars crash and armies fight and die and babies are born and planes fall from the sky and the sea moans and the last drop of water disappears in the desert, but those are no concern to me, because I am witness to something unique, something far more important than having sex with a beautiful English girl who I would eventually disappoint.

I am looking at a kid goat balancing upon the top of a leper's head and they are both smiling in the breaking sunlight.

The English volunteer and I touch for a final time when she shakes my hand goodbye. True, I leave dissatisfied in that painful way known to all of the sexually frustrated, but it really doesn't matter. I want to know if there are further things in life that can compare to Ranadip and the baby goat at dawn.

The girl escaped me, but the leper fell into my arms.

I begin to think there is more than just drinking, running away, lying, sex, and arguing. A dream of the leper and the goat comes to me every few nights. I am possessed by the vision. Nothing else matters. The words I speak during the day are dust. My staff begins to think my malaria has relapsed.

In a trace, the question comes: Can the blood of my life write silent poetic images and add to the science of me? It is an odd thought, but one that seems to fit this phase of my time on Earth.

During a trip to Dhaka, I get an answer to my esoteric wondering.

I turn and look at my driver, the Hindu with the broken teeth. I had not been very sympathetic toward him since that night in the jail. The head driver is suspicious that he is stealing little bits of wire, tubes, and springs from our new engines and replacing them with other, older bits of wire, tubes, and springs. There is always a market for anything glittery in Bangladesh. I wonder to myself if he really is a thief. Does it matter?

At this moment, however, he is doing a great job of driving, crook or not. He guns his way through the slightly less than 100 million Bangladeshis who are trying to block our vehicle. He takes a long, centrifugal turn away from the middle of the road and we suddenly find ourselves upon the edge of the Brahmaputra, son of Brahma.

Suicide and the floating dead don't come to me this time as I gaze out at the perfectly smooth water. Instead I hear something. The river is chanting a song that colors our bodies with the light of the sunset. There are thousands of people along the banks of the river. They are bathing and singing.

"Look," the driver says "they are finding god in the water, Astami Snan, very good."

It is a local Hindu festival tolerated in the midst of an Islamic state and I watch the driver's face as it seems to be absorbing the dye of the fading light much more than mine.

His fate is spelled out in Sanskrit letters along the furrows of his brow. The words are written in five shades of red. It is a language that I don't understand and one that he believes has given birth to everything; the verses of the song lay upon his forehead like a fine string of Burmese rubies.

I look deeply into the refracted images of the stones. Some have stars shining outward. I see old naked holy men dancing down dusty roads. They are alive and beautiful and tragic for the world to see.

Up ahead the hallucination becomes real. Beside the road I see a naked fakir covered in red mud. A group of disciples sit in a semicircle. He holds a stick with an alms bowl tied to it. His penis appears to drag the ground. He is whirling as he jumps and leans in the sooty haze. He waves to me as I pass and I can see that his hand is deformed with what looks like leprosy.

My driver says in a low voice, "I know that man. He is assassin from my village. A most devilish man. He is sadhu now, holy man."

"But he's a killer?"

My driver smiles broadly as his voice rises in excitement. "Yes. You travel through many gates, revealed in many mirrors before you reach paradise, before you are clean. He saw you. You saw him. It will help you."

I look out over the wide, holy river and feel the pressure of three thousand years of Indian history settle down upon my head like the four tiny hooves of a spotted kid goat.

Suddenly I grow hot with commitment. My future is in my imagination. If I am ready, my mind will guide me. I can reflect myself through the passing mirrors of my damaged life and come out unpolluted at the end.

I decide that rare poetic moments shall become my nature and I will search for them and I will find them and I will remember them and string them together like the rubies connecting the temples of my happy driver.

I guess the Brahmaputra, son of Brahma, can wait for me since it knows no time other than oblivion. One can never be late with that kind of a schedule. As we drive next to the river I feel the irregular beating of my heart and the passage of my breath in and out of this world and for the first time in a long time I am happy.

If my plan had worked out, I would have always slept in a bed with fifteen H'Mong and their dogs or spent all my afternoons arguing with my communist friend in Pokhara watching the sun burn the Fishtail or drifted down a jungle river with a bunch of pirates or walked the whore infested streets of Calcutta for eternity or played cards with corrupt Thai policemen or looked down upon a green grass yard while a cobra chased a woman hanging her clothes on a clear African day. But then, that plan didn't work out. I have lost my way. I have responsibilities. I will not end my days on an island in a dirty white suit, barefoot with a bottle of gin in my hand, welcoming the boat from the mainland. My intractable amoebas have discharged. It just didn't happen and sometimes I sit around whining about the whole thing to myself. Sometimes I forget where I am and start speaking out loud. People say what? I usually respond with nothing. But what I really mean is everything.

MEXICO

IN MY MEDICAL OPINION

I AM A DOCTOR, but without formal training. No debts, no degrees, no late night studying, nothing of that nature. My education came the old fashioned way, by self-diagnosis, self-medication, playing with myself, and listening to my sick and injured body.

Sometimes my physique screams at me so it is not hard to hear. Other times it whimpers from the little cracks of my repose. Whenever I confer with so-called real doctors, they get angry. They don't recognize my talents and find me irritating, but that's okay. I know someday when we meet in the high ranging Medical Hall of the Mountain Kings, they will recognize their mistake and I will forgive them with a sprinkling of minute gold idols.

The opinions I hold about medicine and health have been tested. I would put my qualifications up against any doctor who has barely been able to graduate from a small medical school in Dumpsville,

since most of those doctors have never self-diagnosed up a river or
deep in a jungle or out on a desert or in a war zone. It helps to treat
malaria, dengue, typhoid, cholera, and parasites if you have had them.
That is my case before the board of inquiry.

I am currently treating an Austrian lawyer, a Japanese artist, a
teacher from Tennessee, a local gang leader, a street clown, my wife,
son, two dogs, and a Mexican cab driver.

Here is my professional resume:
1) I began my studies as a medical marvel in San Saba, Texas. I was
   born on a kitchen table inside a hospital that looked like a small
   house. A few hours before I came into the world, a tornado hit
   town. The wind scattered dead dogs up and down the street. The
   pound took a direct hit. My weight on the scale was 12 pounds 10
   ounces. The doctors had to remove part of my mother from my
   mouth as they pulled me out with the horse tongs.

2) By six-years old I had organized my female peers into a private
   school of nurses. I sent them into the kitchens of their mommies
   to steal butcher knives for surgery. The knives were stacked in
   the crawl space under my house where the operations were
   performed. When the girls watched me work, they sat in a circle
   with bated breath like naïve, mute students. Above the theatre table
   they grimaced as I made incisions like twenty feet of blood alley.

3) Anatomy was an early specialty. Since I was the only boy on the
   block, I had exclusive rights to play doctor with the nurses. Most
   of them had serious conditions. Stereotypical sexism was rampant
   during this time and I don't recall that any of the girls wanted to
   become "male" doctors. They were happy to be nurses and clean my
   wounds. Playing with ourselves was also part of the curriculum
   and we researched the topic in the quiet libraries of the gardens
   and ditches of our homes.

4) As I got older I diagnosed my respiratory system. I confirmed
   minuscule monsters inhabited my lungs. They were clear and hard
   and sometimes yellow. Their attacks were capricious. On the nights
   when they came, I tried to hammer them to death, but they always
   managed to escape into my closet. During this period I learned that
   breathing was a gift from the little monsters and not my right.

5) During my early adolescence I became an expert on sex. I learned about the subject from dirty magazines. The pictures were similar to what existed in expensive medical textbooks, but at one fortieth the cost. Like most poor students, I did my share of stealing these types of educational materials. Sheets and pillows became something like the women I saw in the textbooks. The sexual fantasies of doctors are well known and I added my peer reviewed comments to the literature.

6) I am also a family doctor. My father let me sharpen the hari-kari knives he used to cut the swelling in his wounds. My bed side manner was good for a child. I also became familiar with various narcotic pain medications mixed with alcohol. This sort of medication was a family recipe. Without it, the 50 year draining of his wounds would have been difficult. I used to think of my father as being better than Jesus. If suffering is the criteria, he certainly outdid the son of God.

7) Sports medicine also attracted my interest. I noticed that what athletes considered major injuries, coaches and trainers called "dogging it." This was my first brush with the conflict between patient opinions and those of the professionals. Fortunately, since I became a doctor early on, I always represented my own injuries in the strongest technical language possible.

8) Parasites consider my stomach a holiday. Amoeba have been drilling and eating me for a long time. Once a doctor told me I didn't have worms. After I self-treated myself with poison, I put the eight foot long tape worm that came out my anus into a little white plastic cup and took it to him. I asked for an evaluation of the stool. It came back positive for parasites, with a note that said "not a typical stool sample."

9) I am a man of many colored piss and the dream coat of Joseph has nothing on my stream. Upon my canvases of urinals, toilets, trees, and walls the pigments of red, green, orange, white, and the old standby brilliant yellow have turned into masterpieces. Art critics are vocal when I don't flush. I am always on the lookout for blue or black. Blue or black elevates urination to catastrophe and a person with those colors will end up hearing hushed tones in the hallway.

10) Feces is my middle name. Let's just leave it at that along with vomit.

11) The first time people get malaria they think they have the flu, for a few hours anyway. The second time it comes, people say, "Shit, I think I have malaria." After three or four discrete cases the symptoms are unmistakable and immediate curatives need to be taken if available. Without a counteractive you are in trouble. I once delayed treatment and it almost killed me. I developed a 106 degree temperature. Doctors laugh at me when I tell them the story. My friend saved my life by putting me into an ice bath. During my delirium my heart became a giant red jazz drum beating in my ears. The offbeat play attracted Jesus from somewhere down the long hall. I assume he floated towards me on the upward draft of cultural conditioning.

12) I have had dengue fever only once. One eyeball bled. I was confused and thought it was malaria. With dengue you feel like you are going to die, but you probably won't, although maybe you will if you have underlying conditions. I did, but was lucky.

13) Just a few words on malaria and dengue prevention: As you lay in bed after a hard day, mosquitoes love to fly into your ear. You then smash your ear in the hopes of killing them. Mostly this is very inefficient. After you take a swing and miss, turn on the lights. Ninety-five percent of the time the mosquito will be directly above and behind you, either on the wall or the headboard. It will be confused after avoiding a swipe and you should be able to squash it easily. A better way to attack the mosquito is to raise the sheet over your head when you initially lay down. Leave enough space for the mosquito. It will fly underneath the sheet and buzz your ear. When you hear the mosquito, simply drop the sheet and kill the mosquito. You can do this by screaming and jumping up and down on the bed. "Die! Die!" Something like that.

14) I am a heart specialist. Aortal fibrillation can be life threatening. The sound of Orkan rockets descending is like freight cars uncoupling. The loud clang of metal is what woke me up. The two explosions turned my heart into a headless chicken, but I was luckier than the six dead next door. The Croatian and Bosnian

doctors, who I attempted to consult, didn't have much sympathy for me. Neither did the beautiful Italian doctor. When I got the medevac, I went to Houston and before I said anything to the physician, I let him read my resume. He took me seriously. Of course, the 190 beats per minute helped.

15) I fell sixty feet off a cliff in Mexico. I was worried about my dog. The medical marvel of my birth has given way to the medical aftermath of my fall. My back is similar to a sack of frogs squirming around trying to get my spinal column to go amphibian.

16) I remember being in a hot warehouse with a wet cloth on my forehead. I was burning up. The jungle birds squawked outside the window. A pretty, drunken, tribal nurse came to help me. She slipped her hand under the sheet and pressed my hot belly button. I felt like I was six-years old again, playing doctor with my covey of young nurses. Nothing much changes, except our physical condition. I have marked it well in my doctor's book and offer my services to everyone, free of charge.

The nightfall of snow dropped upon us like a curtain. We couldn't see much as we walked back to the conference room. Robyn was from L.A. and she had recently hung out with a bunch of comedy writers and been their gofer: scoring drugs, picking up pizza, and calling party girls. At present she was engaged to a guy from Wisconsin. The light from the window guided us and then we stopped and watched as her fiancé spoke to a room full of counterparts and volunteers. The topic was shallow wells. His mouth moved silently while his arms waved around trying to get his body off the ground. Our hands and breath mixed together and then we were touching each other and she looked over my shoulder at her boyfriend standing a few feet away. She kept fiddling with my hair and stepping upon the voice inside of her heart and then she finally whispered hurt me. Like everyone else we were dying and from that point on until I left the Transkei, our relationship was based firmly upon abuse and a very long list of excuses.

AFGHANISTAN

DEATH TO THE MONKEYS

THE AFGHANS WERE TELLING jokes. They were laughing like the war didn't exist and some of their friends weren't being kidnapped and held in little rooms and tortured and finally taken out into a ravine and shot in the head because they had talked to a Westerner; someone like me.

One of the funnier jokes went like this: "Did you see that frog down by the lake? When the wind blew, it jumped into the water and a limb way up on top of the tree moved right at the same time the frog jumped."

Boy that was a killer. Their heads turned full circle in laughter as their beards flung out from their faces searching for a good exorcist. We were sitting around with our shoes off on a carpet drinking tea and eating lousy cookies. Our feet stank like the marching armies of Alexander the Great.

Getting in the mood of the party, I told them the funny, but insightful story of the three wise monkeys: see no evil, hear no evil, and speak no evil. They thought that was hilarious.

I got out my camera. I told the doctor from Paktia to put his hands over his eyes; the engineer from Jalalabad to put his hands over his ears; and the obsessive compulsive jihadist from Logar, who was also my sincere counterpart, to put his hands over his mouth.

I took the photo.

Years later I would pull it out and contemplate how the doctor had murdered the engineer. They also tried to kill my counterpart, but he used the influence of his big time commander brother to buy time. He finally got political refugee status from the U.N. They flew him out of Peshawar on a Fokker. He ended up in Washington D.C. hiding behind his locked door on 14th Street with his six kids and wife.

The three wise monkeys had failed the Afghans. In fact, I heard that the Afghan fundamentalists, the ones who were really close to

God, blew them up just outside Khost in an act of national bravery against a girl's school.

They poured lye into the ears of all the little girls. They didn't want them listening to anything except a mullah reading the Koran. This was actually a small victory. They could have blinded them and cut out their tongues as well.

I guess the monkeys have little chance against the ways of an angry God. That is really too bad for all the Afghans who just might want to hang out with the monkeys for a few lifetimes or even longer.

So much for the lessons taught by the mystic monkeys of long ago.

We couldn't live without Don Guermo, the local pharmacist. His family sat on the little grass strip in front of the curbside business. The Don had a neon sign that said, Vaya Con Don Guermo, La Farmacia Super. Dogs crouched behind the counter where he served his products. He brought the valium and speed out on a little silver tray with a small Dixie cup of cold water. Doug and I always got the "to go" pack. Don Guermo placed it in little brown envelopes and we'd get home to see what surprises were inside. He offered Placydyls, Mandrex, and Vitabolic, all produced in low quality labs from the darker parts of the city. Pharmaceuticals were cheaper than beer or coffee and certainly cigarettes. One day the gunfire was extended. I jogged to the corner next to the university and found a car in the middle of a deserted intersection. It was rolled up against a concrete island with a door open and the engine still running. It was full of bullet holes. A few craning students stood down the street. I looked inside the car and saw the driver and passenger shot to shit. The guy in the back seat was my dentist who also happened to be the head of the national university. My two front teeth were his doing. He'd done a nice job. I was in the wrong place at the wrong time and slowly walked away. Later that night I went to a party, then another one a few days later. From the comfort of smoky rooms we discussed the bombings and kidnappings and assassinations. The students who came to these gatherings were very political. We'd talk about how the Right would kill a priest and the Left would kill a businessman. Everyone agreed the Right was better at the job. Their statistics were more impressive, proving once again the positive correlation between number of guns and number of deaths. Our days passed in slow motion or frenetic jags or mellow hallucinations. Beautiful and handsome left-wing students would nod in the corner or fuck on the couch. We hid behind our green door and listened to the bullets slap through the banana stalks of the plantation above our home. Things were bad in those days, but not so bad that you couldn't get high and cause the chaos to glow along the edges. Witnessing horror while dazed or on amphetamines was apparently part of the university curriculum and some of the young party veterans eventually picked up guns and started fighting. Most of them got killed and with that the party was over.

EL SALVADOR

CHRISTIAN GIRLS DO OTHER THINGS

I WAS TRAVELING with a juicy Christian girl who wanted to get a taste of my life. Although she was very good looking, I thought of her more as a sister than a lover.

We took a vacation to El Salvador during the national elections. I was getting over malaria and amoebas. A few days of sun and fun during what could prove to be violent elections and maybe a coup seemed like an odd tonic, but I thought it was just what I needed. Anything was better than the jungle. I wanted to smooth over the toast of my body with cheese pupusas and cold curtido.

One of my coworkers had said that once we got to the soccer stadium we needed to stay away from the track, lay down in the middle. He had been held in Chile during the Allende coup, so he knew all about the extrajudicial use of stadiums. Latin American dictatorships loved to use them like big open air prisons and the passageways and locker rooms were perfect for enhanced interrogations.

Our trip was sort of like a hurricane party. At most I thought we might get caught in some demonstrations or even riots, but what I had in mind was looking down on the chaos from our fancy hotel room. "Here comes the tear gas. Do you think they're going to open fire? Bring me another drink." Compared to the past four years, it seemed things were getting better in the country. The improvements had been extracted like organs from the dead and missing. In this election all the signs pointed toward the CIA finally backing a winner who didn't track blood when he walked.

When we got off the airplane we passed all the American dependents that were being evacuated out of the country. Kids were laughing and tossing their blond hair around like free tickets to good times, mothers were clean and pretty. Four or five journalists milling near customs were being grilled by armed men in crisp military uniforms. Nobody looked very happy in that group.

The airport was new and I got confused. We left on a slow watermelon truck with a very nice guy who dropped us at the central market. His young helper rode with me in the back, while the Christian girl chatted up in the cab.

Once I got my bearings, we passed the red light district where the women were kept like animals inside cages and then on to the Hotel Ritz. The death squads were known to hang out in the Ritz, but it offered cheap, clean rooms. We took a deep breath and passed the horror of the coffee shop and the killer vanilla custard and went over to the front desk.

When you visit places like El Salvador, you invariably end up walking on the dead and touching the remnants of terrible crimes that might have the name of your country stamped all over them. You are like a child playing on the green grass of an old battlefield still littered with ordinance. Sometimes naiveté can get you through.

I wanted to show my traveling companion the Plaza La Libertad where the soldiers cut down about 1,500 students with rifles and machetes. After that we would head to Hospital La Divina Providencia. Father Romero had been shot in the heart while giving mass at the little chapel inside the hospital. I also wanted to take her up to Puerto del Diablo and show her where the bodies were dumped. How the flowers bloomed so well. Later in the week we'd head to the coast.

We were the only foreigners out and about. The crowds were generally tranquil. We were stopped only three times by soldiers; twice on the bus and once on the street. Each time we said we were late for an appointment with the Ambassador at the U.S. Embassy. They never separated us, which in El Salvador was a good thing. During the stops we wished each other good luck.

The election came and went. The right wing lost and the moderate candidate won. Even though there was an alcohol ban, I hit my old pharmacy for some Vitabolic diet pills and then found a hotel bar that served expats.

Like people with nothing to lose, we hitchhiked down to the sea. We made it to the little hotel and it was just as I had remembered it. We sat on the covered patio and downed a bottle of rum and fresh limes. The waves broke perfectly just off the jetty and the sun went down dreaming of a better future.

We took one of the rooms with twin beds and later that night the girl asked if I wanted to come over to her area, where it was cooler. I said that if I did something like that I was afraid her vagina would start singing like the Book of Psalms, and I couldn't carry that tune. She said Christian girls did other things and I should slip under the covers and find out.

I lay there considering my options and finally told her thanks for the offer, but we had better not. She answered with silence and snoring. Years later I saw her name posted underneath a job advertisement for a Christian aid agency. She was an upper-level manager.

I wrote her a cover letter with my resume attached. About half way down I mentioned that I still regretted not sleeping with her on our El Salvador vacation. A few weeks later I got a form letter that said the job had been given to another candidate, but that they would keep my resume on file. Her signature was at the bottom. It was in red ink and looked like drops of blood.

The French nurses hid in their rooms. Basically they hated me. I had wounded one of their own and they were circling, freezing me out. I sat silently in the living room and then moved onto the porch. Parrots tortured each other with tiny hammers in the trees. A young woman came rolling down the trail in front of the house. She moved with a three thousand year old sway that could have caused the erection of a minor temple, the kind with phalluses for columns. Her face and body were beautiful and I had seen her in the village a few days before. She stopped and called to me. I walked down and yelled back at the house, catch you guys later! A curtain moved *inside and I imagined them looking at me with eyes preparing to send blunt messages to the capital about my character: wanders around naked, uses drugs, steals, etc. I got drunk with the tribal girl and we ended out in the jungle having sex beneath a seasonal waterfall. The explorer Richard Burton was there with field glasses as well as the old Arab slavers from the north and even an oil surveyor with wads of cash to pay off the locals and all together we continued the tradition of discovery and unfair advantage. I left a few days later on a truck filled with big machine retreads. My place in the well-kept history of four French nurses was secure. Still, we were strangers. They knew me about as well as I knew myself, which meant they were operating in the dark, stubbing their toes occasionally on who I was. It seemed to me their sympathies had been misplaced on their friend. They had no idea about how she had tried to remove the oxygen from the air surrounding my head. Or maybe they did and I was just some stupid American guy they enjoyed crapping on. Yeah, that was probably it and they definitely had the stupid American guy in complete focus.*

THE SUDAN

THE PUBLIC HEALTH OF MURDER

THE RIVER LOOKED like a movie screen showing an old Tarzan film. Johnny Weissmuller was one hundred feet tall as he stood upon the surface with his hand cupped around his mouth getting ready to call the jungle. Little huts lined the riverbanks and naked boys poling tree boats glided silently in the fading light.

A blonde under short term contract bathed in an old bathtub on a little dock. She looked at the river and watched the heads of a few crocs disappear and a snake ripple the water on his way to eat a bird. A few thirsty prey animals took a big chance on a cool drink.

Bit, the young Koma slave girl, walked along the bank with Little Sister, who was not really her sister, but she called her that anyway. They wore white slips and their naked breasts moved in time to the influence of their hips.

"Why are you going?"

"He offered me two cans of beer," said Bit. "Mzungu beer."

Her name meant bird in the almost extinct language of her dead parents. They both laughed. Beer was always a good way to start any kind of talk or something more. Bit was interested in the white man. She had only seen a few in her life and she wondered how this one might feel. She wanted to blow the silky strains of his hair with her breath and move them upward away from his eyes.

"You don't think I should go Little Sister?"

"Yes, you need to go, but get more beer. Bring me some. I'm thirsty."

Bit had the kind of puzzling black skin that revealed other color shades when sunlight hit it just right. Sometimes purple or blue came out of the blackness, drawn into the eye like shiny stones at the bottom of a clear stream or the subtle colors of an old portrait when the curtains were finally opened.

Evening spread out and a replacement moon crossed over. They walked for about an hour along the track which bordered the river. Getting lost was impossible, since the soles of Bit's feet were like two maps of Africa.

The left foot was the Sudan and the right foot was Ethiopia.

Sometimes Bit would sit and turn her feet toward her head and look at all the places she had been. The lines, cracks and calluses were villages, rivers, lakes, and trails. As long as she could wash her feet, she knew where she was, where she was going.

You didn't need a map for the Sobat River path. It was well known to everyone, cut by the marching of 350,000 displaced from Ethiopia. When the communist government of Mengistu had fallen, the allies of the Sudan People's Liberation Movement were forced out of Ethiopia and back into the Sudan. The Arabs bombed them as they fled along the Sobat River and occasionally a lion dragged one of them off into the bush, but now they were near the U.N. camps and they had some sense of security, even if it was false.

At last Bit and Little Sister came to the edge of the U.N. compound.

"Should I wait?" asked Little Sister.

Bit shook her head and they both looked at the tent staked near the river's edge. It was away from the outer ring of the U.N. compound, a fair distance from the central cluster of tents and partly destroyed buildings. Both girls wondered silently why the white man with furious blue eyes had chosen to pitch his tent outside the circle of fences and walls. There were lions and snakes about.

Light flowed out beneath the bottom edges of the tent like the liquid of golden beer. Bit squeezed Little Sister's hand and walked away.

"Don't forget my beer," said Little Sister. Her words skipped away down the river and into the reeds.

Bit and Little Sister got their beer. The man in the tent had rough sex with Bit that night and she found out about his hair and body. His skin reminded her of the hot sand desert where she had once wandered for days without water.

When she left the tent she was exhausted and immediately jumped into the river. She felt lost as she swam in the morning light.

If I had known about the sweet personalities of Bit and Little Sister perhaps I would have been even more frustrated and mad. Fortunately, for me anyway, they remained ghosts and only half formed in my imagination. They were little more than transparent victims. Certainly they were real enough, but I had no idea about their pain as they weakened and finally fell.

The letter rested on the desk in front of me. Other problems were raging, but I knew that I had to take the time to deal with what was in the letter.

Outside I watched a Nairobi rainstorm pound my office into submission.

The Indian landlord had done a terrible job with the roof repair. Leaks were everywhere while sheets of solid water moved sideways in the backyard. There was nothing to do except put out pans. My feet were propped up on the desk, above the growing puddles.

I was waiting for the rain to stop and for a German by the name of Jürgen to arrive. He was the director of a small aid agency and we were sometimes in competition for funding. Our contempt for each other had grown into a weak familiarity that supported superficial relations. I had pulled the rug out from under him on a few occasions and gotten grants he was counting on.

He didn't like me. It was that German hate for America thing and I had responded with that America hate for German thing. We were mutually excluding each other.

One of my staff had sent me the disturbing letter. It was about a man named Alfred. He worked for Jürgen's small NGO which specialized in refugee community health.

My own activities were a bit more complex. The agency I worked for was spread across the Horn of Africa dealing with famine in Somalia, war in the Sudan, refugees in Kenya, and now mass exodus from Ethiopia. Staff worked in twelve different sites. On paper our programs were meant to target more than two million people who apparently were all dying and somehow I was partly to blame.

My hair was on fire. At night I dreamt of wild dogs chasing me down the street ripping at my ass. I hung up on interviews with journalists from the states. I always claimed bad connections. There was not much I wanted to tell news reporters. They could never understand. One had to live out here to really know, otherwise, it was like telling stories to tourists and anyway when I tried to speak to journalists I couldn't get the words out.

I was having a small breakdown, just like my secretary Alice.

She had been weeping earlier and I had sent her home for the afternoon. I had no idea that her mother had committed filicide, murdering Alice's brother. The old woman had taken after the young boy with a machete. A trial was approaching, but Alice had never said a word about it, only cried from time to time and told me she was having "boyfriend problems."

Mzungus, white people like me, were usually idiots in Africa. We wore our stupidity like fancy hats, but for some reason Africans forgave us. Perhaps they did so because of their enduring patience, cured in the warm mud of ancient irony.

I had missed everything about why Alice was upset.

The rain finally stopped. The Indian landlord showed up and we got into an argument. He refused to pay off the losing bet he had made with me about whether or not the roof would leak after he had supposedly fixed it. Not only did he welch on 1,000 Kenyan shillings, but he also demanded I cover the cost of any new work on the overhead sieve masquerading as a roof.

My phone rang. Jürgen was in the lobby.

I greeted Jürgen at the door as the landlord went out cussing me under his breath. "People love me in this town," I smiled to Jürgen. We sat down. "I'm not sure where to start," I said. "It's about Alfred, your health care nurse. Do you know Pete? He's one of our sanitarians." He didn't know Pete.

"Well Pete sent me a letter," I said as the letter levitated just off the surface of the desk. The wind was getting through the cracks in the window as the storm began to stir again.

"It seems Pete and Alfred have been sharing a tent for a month or so and Alfred has been sleeping with refugee women just about every night. A few days ago, Alfred told Pete that he had AIDS and the thing is, he apparently hasn't been using a condom and he has known about his condition for some time."

Many moments are burned into my memory and this was one of them. A lightning bolt hit nearby illuminating the room and then the thunder quickly followed and the rain hurled down from a bomber group of dark, sinister clouds.

Where was the film camera? Did I hit my spot? Jürgen the German was beginning to doubt he really understood English. He wanted out of the movie. He kept hanging onto his hatred for me.

Water dripped on the desk between us.

With a blank look, Jürgen started a halting monologue that my story was probably bullshit and all of his staff had to pass physicals and anyway, this was a confidential personnel issue and he would have to contact his headquarters back in Berlin. He thanked me for my concern.

I felt sorry for Jürgen. It was obvious his brain was not thinking quickly enough about his very weak position. Translation from English to German was going slowly inside his mind. Had we been speaking German I am sure he would have caught on much more quickly.

I began to tell him that if Commander Riak found out about Alfred, he would probably kill him or at a minimum castrate him. And if the U.N. heard about it, there would doubtless be negative financial issues for his agency.

Anyway, the whole thing could be avoided if he got Alfred out by tomorrow. Did he really have AIDS? Was he crazy? None of that mattered. He was a community health worker sleeping with multiple refugee women and told Pete he had AIDS. That part was factual and an immediate medical evacuation was required. The guy needed to be tested. He needed help, shit everybody up there needed help.

I finished with a flourish, "By the way, if he does have AIDS, what do you propose to do about all of the women he might have infected?"

Alfred was pulled out the next day. Pete told me that the night before he left, Alfred got drunk and they found him naked down by the river. He was passed out in the mud. Apparently, he had had sex one last time.

In my poker heart, I knew what Pete wrote was true. The guy had AIDS and was slowly murdering women. I imagined infecting African girls somehow compensated for his bad luck or lousy choices or maybe spreading the disease turned him on in some deviant way.

The irony of a health care nurse being the source of a deadly disease was more than ironic, it was criminal. Maybe I should have sent a message to Riak. I'm sure he would have killed the guy. That would have been a better ending to the story.

I never told anyone other than a few headquarter staff about what had happened. Pete didn't tell a soul, which was a small miracle since he felt partly to blame. For years after he would call me on the phone saying how badly he felt.

Pete did a little checking about whom Alfred might have infected. Trying to track down public health risks in scattered displaced camps was difficult: "I'm looking for some young women who are tall or short and black and dress in old clothes that have slept with a white man." Good luck, pal. He never found the likes of Bit and Little Sister. By the time he got out to their camp, they were gone in one of the migrations that sought lower ground.

I sent Jürgen all the information. I never heard back from him and a few months later he took a job with a private company in Namibia. The Sudan People's Liberation Army split apart. Commander Riak took the lead with one of the factions. Thousands died in the process. The war from the north soon spread down to the area where Alfred had pitched his tent and the whole show began to move toward the Kenyan border. The Toposa tribe eventually flipped for the Arabs and everybody flooded into Kenya and Uganda by the hundreds of thousands.

When new volunteers came out, I'd start by giving them an AIDS talk. I would vaguely reference how easy it was to get it in Africa and that they should always be careful about who they slept with. I told the women to avoid the guys who hung out in the bars and told the guys to stay away from the bars.

I guess Alfred died soon enough. Helpful drugs back then were scarce. I have no idea, but I do know that the AIDS epidemic in Africa swept across the land like the Old Testament was trying to add a new book that would confirm how picky God could be.

In all of this, Alfred had played his role as one of the many angels of death flying around the place, but to give him his due, he was a little different from the others and this particular episode of his sorry life certainly made an impression on me.

The married couple came into my office upset. He was about fifty years old and looked like somebody had switched his head with a skeleton's skull. She was pretty and younger, but her eyes were two black tunnels that had been drilled into the side of a German mountain. There was probably no way out of the darkness once you drove into them. The pair was there to complain about cuts in their project funding. Both were psychiatrists working with rape and torture victims. They explained how large their case loads were and about how much stress they and their patients were under and that the project could not afford to lose support staff or facilities. The man's voice rose in harsh judgment as he spoke and the woman shed a few tears. Professionalism fell across my face and I began to emote like a tired bureaucrat. I sympathized with them, but kept saying my hands were tied and the cuts would take effect in two months. They stared down at the floor and then the man stated for the nightly news that they would be forced to resign. From an attaché case he pulled out two letters. I read them and saw the underlined, bold two week notice. I told them I was sorry and then they left my office. There was a very dark feeling that came over me when they shut the door. I thought I could detect the pattern of a face floating in the air. When I looked closer it was only dust captured in a breaking shaft of sunlight coming through the clouds down into the office. After two weeks they flew home. One month later I got a call from my desk officer in New York. The married couple had committed double suicide in their little house by a lake somewhere in England. I looked out my window and watched the snow fall upon the Balkans as I said, Jesus fucking Christ. The woman on the other end said what? You're breaking up and then I went ahead and hung up.

THAILAND

THE MÉNAGE A' TROIS OF PASSPORTS

PETER AND I WERE deep in the jungle lying on beach towels along a little sandy strip near the water. We were on the Thai side of the Mekong River watching Susan swim to Laos. The Lao usually swam the other way, toward Thailand, away from the communists. It made sense since they wanted to escape and become refugees. When they got to this side they were welcomed by a kind of slow rotting freedom that kept them in the camps for years.

I had dared Susan to try and she smiled as she stripped down. It didn't look that far. I told her I thought I could kick a football across the river. She started strong, but then we watched her struggle when she got about half way across. The current suddenly seemed more like a wave of light or time and little frames of her body clicked across the surface of our eyes.

Peter passed me a joint and we slowly began to understand that we were witness to a remarkable, perhaps even unique, sight. We couldn't do anything but watch and hope for the best.

After about fifteen more minutes of fighting for her life, she finally crawled onto the opposite shore. She collapsed motionless, but in the stands the monkeys, parrots, butterflies and Olympic land mine victims went nuts applauding.

I asked Peter if he had any ideas on how she was going to get back. He shook his head and took another puff from the Thai stick. "She'll figure something out." We continued to watch her long, sexy body stretched out on the rocks as the river flowed over her feet. She seemed motionless and we could not see her back heaving.

Susan and Peter were lovers. Susan and I used to be lovers. We all lay there along the Mekong like a ménage a' trois of trust that had crossed an international boundary without proper documentation. Despite the remnants of the war, we were hopeful the Lao authorities would stamp our love stained passports and forgive a truly great swimming performance by the girl with long legs.

He was a Peace Corp volunteer and worked with fishing cooperatives. On a regular basis one of his friends from San Diego sailed a boat down and waited just off shore so they could meet and exchange frozen shrimp for hand guns. The economics of the operation were admirable. El Salvador shrimp were high quality and plentiful, guns in San Diego were cheap and available. The guns on the black market in El Salvador brought a high price, much more than shrimp. The money from the sale of weapons went back to the fishing cooperative minus a commission to the Peace Corps volunteer and his boat captain pal. It was more than optimal, it was perfect and covered with an American spirit that said when all the people and animals are dead, and the air and water are foul, and the forests and jungles are gone, we will eat our dollars as if they were fresh salad. The volunteer often said he was doing something that dovetailed nicely into U.S foreign policy and he was right. The CIA and U.S. Army were supplying the Salvadoran military and security forces with weapons. At the Plaza La Libertad massacre another volunteer, who had been a soldier, photographed the Salvadoran military firing U.S. rifles into the people jammed up at the church door. The U.S. Embassy at first denied the claim, but after they saw the photos said, "We will certainly check into this." Politics are terrible. Had my neighbor been selling to the Left, I wouldn't have minded so much, but he was selling to people with deep humor deficits that were two dance steps from the death squads. I guess he was smart. By selling to the Right, he got invited to first-rate parties. Supplying the Left would have put him a hole. He often said the guns were for self-defense and I guess on a philosophical level that might have been true. Philosophy, however, was worthless to the students, nuns, priests, campesinos, and workers who took bullets to the brain. Over 100,000 died in the dirty war, most killed with U.S. weapons and their bodies were somehow lost in all of the talk about communists attacking the Texas border and driving deep into the barbeque pits of American backyards.

KENYA

THE GHOST RESCHEDULES

EVERYBODY HAD TO BE somewhere, but the refugee aid director wasn't supposed to be at the party. He should have been up on the border meeting a rebel doctor. As he stood looking at all the people with their mouths open, the change of plans made him feel uneasy like his zipper was down.

A justice of the Supreme Court was being feted with a birthday party at the ambassador's house. The invitation for the director had come at the last second. Suddenly, seeing the doctor on the border didn't seem so important. Tomorrow he would have to send a radio message about the change of plans. The meeting would be a day or two late. In Africa, a delay like that was really nothing.

Due to a list of traumatic reasons, a ghost came into the director's mind and took on a three dimensional shape. Ants were inside the specter's eyes.

"I'll send the radio message," said the ghost. The director smiled, and thought okay, you reschedule the meeting. The haunt disappeared and then quickly returned to a wrought iron table where he sat smoking a sulfur cigarette. It was a game the director often played, designing dead people from the past to advise him, to do his bidding.

This particular ghost face was from a body stuck in the reeds where the director had bathed. The eyes were being eaten by ants that were carrying the flesh up the grass and across a tree limb and finally onto the bank. They moved in a jumbled line like tiny disorganized butchers holding their meat over their heads for everyone to see.

Although the director was the only one invited from his agency, he had brought two party crashers along, a beautiful girl and her obnoxious, handsome husband. They had all met at an exclusive beach resort.

He had been attracted to the woman immediately. Breasts, hips, shoulders, lips, blonde hair all came together to spell money. Not the kind in a wallet, but in trusts or underground. Her immediate assets were long legs and small feet. She was a racer and looked a sure thing over short distances.

She and her husband had been arguing at the bar. When he approached them and offered a round of drinks, they had accepted. As they shook hands, the girl held his eyes too long.

Over the next few days they openly flirted. She suffered under the critical stares of the husband. He often cut her off in mid-sentence and didn't appear to value her mind or body. She retaliated by acting available with other nearby men. Even the pool boys and waiters were caught in the net she continually cast.

The couple, who were in their early thirties, was from the Netherlands and appeared liberated in the rude Dutch way. The husband left the wife alone on the beach for hours. Men hovered around her. Maybe at one time they loved each other, but that promise looked damaged as they consumed quiet food and awkward wines in the expensive restaurant. Their lives were empty and ennui had become a sort of well-dressed companion keeping notes in a dry diary.

The interaction of all three of them excited him. At this stage the director needed dramatic stimulation. They played tennis and went snorkeling together. When they talked about their respective lives the director lied about his age. He looked ten years younger than he really was, so he went with appearance instead of truth.

He tended toward younger women. Yoga, weights, Lady Clairol kept him in the game. He never thought of his situation as sad, but others who knew him did.

At the resort they had discussed the possibility of the couple volunteering in one of his projects. She had been a teacher and had a degree in nutrition. Perfect. The Sudan, Somalia, Rwanda, all were possible sites for her. The husband could work logistics since he used to be in the oil business.

They discussed how it would feel to do something for somebody else. A seed of compassion grew inside the girl, fertilized by the faltering relationship with her husband. "I'd love to volunteer for a few months, maybe longer," she said too enthusiastically.

Volunteers were always needed. They were relatively inexpensive and were vital to implement projects. It was poetry when they took to the field and began to work in the worst conditions.

Good volunteers could put Baudelaire, Eliot, and Coleridge to shame as they wrote lines of tents and stanzas of feeding stations and epics of feeding clinics that rhymed and roamed across the dark masses of the dying to awaken them for one more day of struggle. He had seen more babies saved by this sort of stitched together picture than he cared to remember.

His staff had joined him for many reasons. Some were pure of heart, naive, and wanting to help, others were criminals, drug addicts, drifters, and liars. A good number were skilled professionals who enjoyed solving the kinds of problems that were unavailable back home.

He thought many things of the volunteers who worked under his shaky control. As a general rule, the better looking they were the less impressive their convictions and commitment; too many distractions.

The Dutch girl was emerging as an exception to the rule. He liked how she was, how her smooth brown thighs and knees complimented the short black dress she had chosen for the party. Maybe the commitment part just needed a little water and sunlight, care from a gardener.

Embassy gatherings like this one were usually forced marches through the dismal conversations of people the director didn't like. As he looked around he felt queasy.

He returned his attention to his guests. The husband was frowning. "Why would I want to live in a tent and get sick?"

"Do you always have to think about yourself?" retorted the woman.

The director considered both of them and said, "You're right, of course. I can guarantee the tent and the illness is a real possibility. It's pretty insecure as well."

"Count me out," said the husband, "and I don't want you going either."

"We'll see," she said as she looked at a handsome soldier in a dress uniform.

The husband went to the bar.

"What do you think?" asked the director.

"Where is she," the girl said, referring to the guest of honor. The director had promised an introduction.

"I think that's her, over there," he pointed with his third empty glass.

The director noticed the ghost waving from across the room. Why had he come back into his mind? Something was wrong with the ghost's hand. It was troubling.

The court justice talked and laughed loudly as she downed her drink. Her figure was imposing and she looked as if she were arguing. The director noted she was wasted, but then who was he to judge a judge.

Over the years he had tried to curb his own alcoholism since he was slowly going blind in one eye. A Honduran doctor had once told him that toxic neuritis caused about 3% of all alcoholics to go blind in either one or both eyes. He didn't know if that was true or not.

The ambassador's wife approached like a lioness bowing intently along the tile and took him aside. She was the kind of woman who spoke in complete paragraphs. After a long introduction she asked, "Who are the two uninvited guests?"

There was a major crime to be solved. He apologized and told her he had no excuse, but they were old friends who had arrived at the last minute. He felt obligated to bring them.

She looked at him with the faux pas magnifying glass that the wives of ambassadors had grown onto their hands. To her he looked like a lying bug squirming around avoiding the reality of his disrespect. She finally faked a smile and as she walked away said that she would set two more places at the back.

The justice was wobbling toward him and the Dutch girl. They all introduced each other and then the justice said, "So what do you do?"

The director went blank for a moment and then answered, "I work with refugees."

"Oh," she said. "I want to ask you a question. What is a refugee?"

"Well, it's pretty straight forward." He gave her the stock U.N. definition: a person who is forced out of their country of origin, for a number of oppressive reasons, and who has a fear of returning to that country or who has had their nationality taken from them through oppressive force and then find themselves outside of their country of origin.

She took a sip of her drink and said, "Well, yes, but what is a refugee?"

The Dutch girl, who spoke perfect English, looked at him and waited. "I just told you," he said.

"Not really," she responded.

Okay, fine he thought, as he took a long drink.

"You know a refugee is a lot like pornography. You might think of refugees as the sex actors in a porn film. Everybody gets to screw them."

The ghost suddenly materialized beside the justice. Three of his fingers were bloody stubs. He poked the justice in the side with his elbow. "Can you hear the crying? It's funny!" he shouted with a vile laugh. No one heard the ghost except the director.

The justice didn't miss a beat and said, "When pornography comes before the court, the other justices sit around and watch porn as part of their deliberations. The law clerks keep track of the sex acts in each film; sodomy, bestiality, incest, anal, oral, doesn't matter, they keep count."

"What are you talking about?" asked the husband as he returned from the bar. "It sounds interesting."

"Not really," said the justice.

"I think it is," said the Dutch girl.

"There is something I have always wondered about," said the director looking at the justice.

"And what is that?"

"How would the court look upon autofellatio?"

"Do you mean in a film?" she said.

"No, I was thinking more along the lines of the actual act. Would it fall under the same category as some of the state sodomy laws? Is it like masturbation or is it worse under the law? Would a person performing that deed be breaking the law?"

She drew a look of consternation and as she was about to respond, the wife of the ambassador walked up behind her.

"Yes, you know, sucking your own dick. Would there be a trail? Could you go to jail?" asked the Dutch girl with a laugh.

Horrified, the ambassador's wife took the arm of the justice and pulled her away.

"What are you doing?" asked the justice as she momentarily struggled.

Hundreds of years of diplomatic training moved the ambassador's wife as if she had been frozen in ice waiting for the right emergency to reanimate and save her country. A cold cloud enveloped the two women as they floated toward the dais where black waiters waited to serve a main course of duck slathered in orange sauce.

The ghost watched the guests eat the duck as he swung from the chandelier. He screamed, "I hate my mother!" and then spewed vomit across the crowded room.

After the party, the director drove the Dutch couple to their five-star hotel. The girl was animated and recounted the party and the drunken justice. She raved about the strawberry frappe. The director had thought it looked too much like blood. The husband acted bored and told her he was sleepy.

They decided to take a nightcap in the bar. As they were talking the husband excused himself and went up to his room as he had done so many times at the beach. After he was gone, the girl said she wasn't tired and wanted to see where the director lived. In the car she slid across the front seat and leaned into his body on the curves.

The director wondered if he should take the girl to bed. If she was to become a volunteer, this would ultimately be a problem. She put her hand on his leg and he thought that if she moved any closer he would have no other choice but to have sex with a new volunteer.

After he took her into his bedroom, she began to disrobe. He looked at her without speaking for several minutes. She returned his gaze and then began talking about her philosophy of a free world. The half-formed ideas were resting on the couch of her money. Rich liberals had the time and furniture to think about such things.

"So did you ever do it?"

"Well, yes, when I was younger. It's not so hard if you are flexible enough."

"I think you will be the first man I ever made love with who sucked his own dick. This should be fun."

Her movements were expensive and well-timed. As they made love, the ghost was busy in the bathroom ripping out tiles and calling to animals.

Afterwards they lay watching the overhead fan turn. At about 3:00 a.m., he took her back to the hotel. She said she really wanted to help the refugees and get away from her husband for a while, but there was condescension in her voice.

They made plans to meet, but she ended up leaving that afternoon with her husband for Zanzibar.

When she had entered the hotel room after being dropped off, she found the husband sitting on the bed crying. He told her that he really did love her, but in his own way. His mother was about to die and he would inherit the complicated family businesses. Among other things were retail stores, a corporate health franchising operation, and gold mines. It was a huge responsibility. He wanted her to help him, to keep being his wife. Otherwise, if she really wanted to, she could go live in a tent out on the bush.

It really wasn't much of a choice for her and she decided to keep her designer, impatient marriage.

The justice got up at noon nursing a hangover and left for a new country on her tour of Africa still confused about refugees. The ambassador's wife spread rumors about what happened at the party. She shaded things considerably with the diplomatic ink provided by the state department.

The director never got another social invitation from the embassy. As a consolation, he went down to the store and bought a bottle of Lady Clairol, Ash Blonde, and dyed his hair.

When the director went into the radio room later that day to send the message to the doctor, he was informed that the doctor was no longer in the U.N. compound. The radio operator said that the doctor had wanted to seek refugee status in Kenya. That was why he wanted to meet with the director.

Three days passed and then the ghost, who rescheduled the meeting and swung from the chandelier, delivered a message from the doctor on the border. The news came in a sibilate whisper directly into the director's ear.

The Garang faction had kidnapped the doctor from a shebeen hut near the U.N. camp and tortured, tried, and executed him on the evening of the birthday party for the justice.

With every drink the director finished at the party, the doctor lost a finger. They used a pair of wire clippers. The trial started when the director brought up autofellatio and was over when the ambassador's wife pulled the justice away. With the main course the doctor finally gave up and began to curse his own mother and then vomited. The dessert was the coup de grace and the blood spurted out the doctor's head like the strawberry frappe the Dutch girl sucked into her mouth. They dumped the doctor in a ravine and left him for the animals along about the time the director was having sex.

The ghost was in both places at the same time. Like all of his kind, he was a voyeur and loved to watch the real time decay of the living as they moved into his neighborhood.

The doctor, as the director later recalled in his nightmares, was indeed a bona fide refugee and could have served as a classic example for the justice.

Emergency relief agencies feel obligated to hold coordination meetings. The words spoken in these gatherings can fill all the empty bottles that have ever been cast into the sea. Beachcombers bend over and dig them out of the sand, hoping to find a love letter or plea for help. Instead they read about shared fuel costs and old wheat being turned into worthless currency or mandates that have been defined after weeks of tense interagency negotiation. When the dying begins in earnest, we cover the world with coordination. It gives us something to do while we figure out what to do and then there is a good chance we end up doing nothing. Coordination can pull the skin of a refugee's forehead over his eyes and nose and mouth and then stretch the skin all the way to the floor. When you see the face of a refugee in the newspaper, with that long, sad look, it is because coordination has pulled his skin down to the floor and nailed it there.

SOMALIA

DEATH AND GARBAGE ON THE INTERNATIONAL ART MARKET

THE WORTH OF DYING is variable. Why are the deaths of the dark-skin poor, who live far from oil and with names we cannot pronounce, of a lesser value? Are their smiles different? Maybe it is the way they die; how they fall and rot upon the ground.

Their foreign bones must bleach in a different way and the worms must find their flesh unappetizing. Yes, that must be it.

I am in a camp with pungent odors and clashing colors. It is near a range of mountains where internally displaced people make their way down in long, slow moving lines as if they were blind or suffering from brain concussions. They jam the roads and trails and collapse ever so often and use their short breaths like weak frequencies that pulse unanswered Maydays.

The encampment is tightly packed and the air is stifling. Water is scarce and people live on a gallon or two a day. Shit and garbage are on the ground, while little boys and girls lie in the shadows of huts. I know that in a few weeks the black shade will take them and they will be dead and ready to join the others waiting patiently to disintegrate.

Hundreds die by the day here like a soundless thread of blood slowly snaking its way across the floor.

The feeding station is up ahead. I have been avoiding it on purpose. A few weeks ago I broke down in front of an embassy staffer: nothing major, just a few tears, a little snot, and a quick exit. Reluctantly I enter the makeshift canvas and plastic structure. After a few questions, a nurse, who doesn't like me, puts a dead baby in my arms and tells me to take the body behind a curtain. I find a bed with ten lifeless children, each neatly wrapped and snuggling into the end. The flies are everywhere. As I leave, I vow never to return. The nurse is hooked on Vicodin and I am tolerating it, but still, we don't mix very well.

She thinks I hate women, which is an odd thought, even one clouded by addiction. I figure she doesn't know that I have spent most of my life worshipping women, since they are obviously better than men.

Usually you don't find groups of women with guns blasting everything in sight, setting up torture rooms, and planning the annihilation of cities or countries or entire ethnic populations. Most women just don't think that way. The nurse will never know my feelings and how I'd like to put women in charge of the important stuff. Give them a chance for a while. Men are driving the whole thing directly into radioactive brick walls that explode upon impact.

At night and in the morning as thousands of the displaced stir in their tents and cardboard boxes, the stages of history shift into one of the lower gears. The sound is strained as the crest of the next hill waits.

Groups of irregular soldiers stand smoking cigarettes, leaning on their weapons waiting for halfcocked orders. When the darkness comes, they go into the camp and drag women out and have their way with them. Usually they are high on something, but right now they look sober.

A cluster of thin-as-glass-sheet Somalis are resting under a dry tree. The damaged shadow looks thirsty. Behind their closed eyes they are dreaming of a cool bath and fresh fruit. Three kids are kicking an old soccer ball and a pack of dogs fight in the dust.

Triple-priced melons are being pitched from the back of a trader's truck and stacked near the piles and piles of stinking garbage. Only a few have enough money to buy any of the melons. Regardless of how bad a famine is, there is always food around for the wealthy who can afford to pay pirate prices.

Maybe a week earlier, we carried a woman out of the garbage pile near my tent. She must have died while searching for something, anything. She obviously wasn't part of the melon market. I vaguely remember hearing sounds scratch around, but I thought a night dog was visiting.

Somalis are rich in the colors of light, but not much more. The kaleidoscope of their traditional clothing swirls down the lines of the infant feeding stations and into the cots of the hospital tents and overlays the chaos of the food distribution.

The brightness of the light forces me to wear sunglasses during the day and night. It is too intense for me. I am drowning in colored light. It is all around me and I am sharing it with a million Somalis.

If only Monet were here to paint this scene, this vast tragedy, for the entire world to see. If the masterpiece hung in a museum then everyone could gaze, transfixed at the garbage and the death and it would become a much-admired French classic.

The painting of the dark-skin dead and the garbage they pile upon their misery could be bid up by anonymous buyers on the international art market. At the final sale, the well-dressed auctioneer might magically turn the proceeds into potable water.

Perhaps art is the solution to the variable value of death or maybe there's no hope and I need to forget about it; lie down with the empty bottles in my tent and think about something else. Yeah, get my mind off of things and watch the rape victims, now labeled as whores, walk arm-in-arm along the road with slow, dusty steps.

I was hitting a few bars. A new short-term contract in a real shit hole was coming up and I wanted to get laid. As I entered into a place owned by an old acquaintance, I saw a group of good looking women drinking at a table. They seemed vaguely familiar. I sat beside them and ordered a margarita.

Screwing up the courage to meet a new Pandora, my ears began hearing a story from my past. One of them said you know Ginger was really wasted. She had been drinking all night and when we got to the club she took one shot and then slipped off her chair. We let her lay there in that horrible red dress with the fish on it. She was so really gone. When we left we rolled her against the wall and tipped the waiter. We had to step over her to get out. The women didn't look so pretty anymore. They all began to laugh and I downed my drink and left. As I drove away I recalled Ginger and the red dress with the fish on it that I had bought her in Puerto Escondido. We had gone there running away from our scheduled wedding that her parents had organized like a political election. The Catholic priest had known I was a loser at playing Texas. I could see her there against the wall like a collapsed bridge that used to connect her body to a bunch of dreams. She was a beautiful, wild girl and had remained frozen in my mind at twenty-five when we were together naked on white sheets in cold air conditioning, burning into each other's body. She used to get out a plastic ruler and measure my dick. She'd make it hard and then I'd force it up as high as I could, but it was never enough for either one of us. Then she'd size the width and we'd laugh and then I'd turn her over for a good time. Smiles, money, hopes and dicks can never be too big. Our marriage, had it happened, would have been a giant bonfire burning in the mountains along the border. The Mexicans on the other side would have confused our distant flames with the return of Emiliano Zapata and a new round of awful fighting. They would have assumed Zapata had taken over Ginger's 20,000 acre goat ranch and thrown all the gringos into the river.

THE MIDDLE EAST

TWO BULLETS

THE DIRECTOR HAD shocking red hair, was nearsighted, overweight and in a bad marriage. His wife and four kids were unhappy with him. They cussed him openly, but he barely heard their muffled voices. Most of their complaints centered on money, games, clothing, and pizza.

At night he drank Dutch beer and watched Sky porn. The more beer he drank, the better the porn looked. He spent most of his days playing video games for hours at a time. He would tell his secretary he didn't want to be disturbed and then he'd move little robots through a maze while rockets rained down on his computer screen. In the great mix of things, none of these behaviors were too unusual, except he was the head of a multimillion dollar emergency relief operation in a war zone.

He was on the verge of going insane, but he kept those offbeat feelings chained to a malnourished female dog in his mind. He enjoyed petting her when everything got very still. When he talked to the dog he sounded like a mechanic using makeshift tools on an old broken down car.

He never bothered to feed the bitch, but she still responded to his metallic words with hope. She smelled inside his heart with her nose down; searching for bones to lick that might be jammed in the dark pumps.

A sniper had taken two shots at the director while he drove alone toward a project site. The shooter was about 500 meters away in a building.

The first shot came through his windshield and the second one hit the headrest on the passenger's seat. He had managed to swerve off the road and stop behind a garbage dumpster.

He visualized his brain splattered in the vehicle when the bullets found their mark. Not doing his job grew out of those vivid images. They also crept into his nightmares and he began to think of himself as more dead than alive.

When he sat down to "do some work" everything was weighed against that minute on the road. As he tried to write or sit in a meeting, his mind kept coming to the conclusion that nothing mattered more than his own life.

From that realization he began to justify and obfuscate.

Reports went undone or sent late. Rudeness marred his relations with staff and their oversight became non-existent. The various project sites, spread across a four country region at war, began to go wrong. Staff morale fell precipitously. He broke promises easily and lied when it suited him.

This went on for months. Staff would confront him and he would fire them. Headquarters supported him in all his actions.

One day the chief accountant came into his office. On a number of different issues the accountant had followed his lead. He left work early, called in sick, took tranquilizers, and had connected a wire between their computers that allowed them to jointly play games.

"I have some bad news," the accountant said. "We are one million U.S. over budget."

"Are you sure?"

The accountant drew in a breath and squinted. "Well, I'm pretty sure. The site accounts are a mess. We're six months behind on those, but if I make estimates on past expenses and project to the present, it seems pretty clear that we're over."

"Jesus. Why did you do that?" asked the director.

"I don't know. I just got to thinking about it."

"Is it really that bad? One million?"

"I would say that one million is on the conservative side. It's probably more like $1.5 million."

"Who else knows?"

"Just you and me," said the accountant.

"And you're sure about this?"

"Well, more or less. You know how it is."

"Okay, let's put a lid on it for now. I need to take care of a few things," he said.

The only thing left for the director was to tell his secretary he didn't want to be bothered by anyone, no calls, and no staff meetings. He locked his door and returned to his video games. After a few hours, which included setting new high scores for monster kills and spaceship destruction, he left for home.

His wife and kids were visiting relatives. He filled an ice container with beer and turned on the Sky porn. He played with himself for a while, switched to a war movie, kept drinking, and then along about 1:00 a.m. he passed out.

Later that morning, while he was sleeping off the Dutch beer, a rocket fell on the city. The explosion killed 65 people and wounded 131.

In England, at the same time the rocket hit, an accountant was preparing a bill on the Sky satellite account of the director. Two months

behind in his payments, Sky terminated his services that day. The
porn died as a woman opened a door with her vagina.
   The tragedies mounted for the director. The home office called and
left a message that an auditor was coming out. Six of his field staff
resigned. His wife drained their bank account and took the kids on an
extended vacation. Then one afternoon he locked himself in the office
bathroom. He turned off the lights and sat on the toilet for 14 hours.
   His starving dog lay at his feet in the dark. Her eyes warmed him
like two burning coals. They conversed all night and he cut open her
stomach and placed springs and levers into her intestines. In the
morning he heard knocking and the voice of his secretary.
   "Is anyone in there?"
   His first reaction to the question was that he didn't know, but he
managed to move his feet and hands. The dog growled. He cracked
the door to see her smiling face outside his sanctuary. He fumbled
for something to say. What could save him he wondered?
   "Do you need anything?" she asked. He didn't answer, but only
sat back down on the toilet and listened to the sound of her footsteps
fade away as he petted his dog.

   *All of my friends in El Salvador were miserable. Except if they were rich
and beautiful. Then they had the world by the balls. Otherwise, the ones I knew
in the streets or down in the barrancas had problems that started with the teeth
and the feet. The teeth were black with decay and the feet were bloodied with
sores. When the poor of El Salvador ate they could not chew. The food disappeared
down black holes in their jaws, where their teeth should have been, and then it
continued to fall through their bodies and out the open sores of their feet and
landed upon the ground. The Salvadoran earth was being fertilized with food
and blood. It was why the plants were green. It was why everyone was so thin
and small. As the Salvadorans continued to diminish, I understood how the
organic specks of the people could actually float up into the sky and ride on the
wind and get stuck onto the surface of clouds. Being part of a rainstorm was
surely an improvement over what the earth offered. Standing in a Salvadoran
downpour was like feeling the rush of a million people wash over your body.
Each drop was the smiling face of a person happy with their new home in the*

sky. Yes, the smiling face religion would be a cleansing tonic for the people of El Salvador and I couldn't wait to take a shower in my courtyard with some of my female converts. We could clean or souls and suds up our private parts.

TEXAS

REMEMBERING

CARS DRIVEN BY UNHEALTHY PEOPLE sat in the parking lot of a restaurant that specialized in butter biscuits covered with chicken fried bacon and white gravy. I was arguing with three enormous men who apparently had feeding tubes running between the kitchen and their bowels. They were rig workers in the "ow n ga bine."

I was lost and needed directions, but somehow had found the time to debate idiots about Africa.

The fat men said crazy things, like Texas was larger than the Sudan and that during the summer Alaska melted down making Texas the biggest state in the union. One of them said, "Now look, okay boy, I'll give you this, the whole place of Africa is about three times the size of Texas, but just barely."

The others frowned with the lips of dead Confederates. Racist and ignorant words floated on the silence; old vocabulary that seemed lost and dying, like sick birds hiding in the shadows of scrubby brush.

"Get your facts straight," one of them growled at me.

I was on home leave, near the town of Dime Box, which was near Old Dime Box. The dimes, stacked in little boxes, were setting inside the houses of the two towns waiting for someone to take them out and make change. The coins were for postal stamps and had been placed there by old people with tiny holes in their pockets. The boxes were cheaper than new pants.

I finally got my directions and started driving. The land was covered in hay and cows and horses and feral cats and dogs. The sun burned down and the land whispered that it could take it and would be there just like that forever.

It was wrong, of course, and the future held thousands of dead oaks, drought, wildfire, plant disease and the end of dry land farming which would ironically turn parts of Texas into a landscape similar to the Sudan.

I was trying to find an old coach of mine. My goal was to replace what I had just been through with something new by way of my past. It was a process I went through after each assignment.

I'd put on my archaeologist clothes and dig up home ground and dust off images of my youth. It helped me to stabilize my body, to prevent a collapse in public places. I had been known to start crying for no apparent reason or mutter to myself loudly. People thought me weak or unbalanced and I guess I was both.

My coach was in poor health and I wanted to find him before he disappeared. The death of his wife had made a very large impact upon me when I was younger. She was the home economics teacher and after she found out about the affair, she drank an entire bottle of whiskey and hung herself.

The sheriff had found her naked, dangling in a door frame like a woman, as he said later, who had known what she was doing.

I first met her in typing class. She had coal black hair, blue eyes and nice legs. I remember being attracted to her in that shy furtive way just past puberty. It was new to me being interested in an older woman who drank coffee, left lipstick on cigarette butts, and crossed her legs in a way that distressed me like injured butterflies slowly moving their wings on the ground. There was not much I could do about it but suffer along with the butterflies.

At the end she was drinking the fifth and walking around the house slowly stripping, crying, cursing, hoping the liquor would force the Earth to reverse its rotation and back everything up to a night before the younger woman had come along; a safe night covering her marriage, where she could hear his soft breathing and stretch her arm out across his chest and slowly fall asleep upon their bed and then the planet could start turning in the right direction again and move along a path where she would be smarter and closer to him. She couldn't stop thinking that some of this was her fault, maybe the biggest part.

On cold winter's days I would walk with my dog on the college campus by my home and think about her trying to reverse time as she fumbled in the dark tying the knot, faulting herself, losing her life in those minutes before it was lost.

It was my first thoughtful lesson on the consequences of our actions.

I had played four years of different sports under my coach. When he got mad at me he threw his watch against the wall or kicked a basketball the length of the court or took a bat and hit the backstop. Sometimes he grabbed my face mask and swung me around like a cat.

There was once a perfect day on new spring grass. He was hitting me bloopers in the outfield. Every so often he shouted to hustle up and then I yelled back that someday I was going to Africa and he shouted why would I want to do that and I ran in shagging balls and said breathlessly that I wanted to live in every country in the world and since Africa had the most countries that I wanted to start with Africa and he said but why leave Texas?

He swept his arms around toward the pasture across from the baseball field and we looked at the cows ruminating on cud. "Isn't it beautiful?"

As I drove down the narrow dirt roads I looked for a shabby little white house sitting in a pasture that was fenced with barbed wire and cedar posts. Since most of the houses around there fit that description it took me a while before I drove up to the right one.

Howling Red Bones, Blue Ticks and one old Bloodhound surrounded my car and then at the screen door an old man appeared in a bathrobe. It was him.

We sat in his living room. He had the expression of a defeated general reading the terms of surrender. The air was full of old skin cells floating around and I tried not to breathe.

Half-filled bottles were slanting against things and he was just finishing a white bread baloney sandwich. I declined food, but said yes to a drink.

I asked him how he was doing and he said he was doing as well as an 85-year old man with a bad stomach could be expected to do. "How many men my age do you know walking around having a good time?"

Our conversation dipped into the past and he brought me up-to-date on my old friends who were still living in the area. He told me about the plumbers, cops, teachers, and carpet layers who used to be my teammates. Some were happy, some not. Many had kids, most went to church, and others were drunks. He knew all the small town tales about people spinning in one spot, caught in the eddies of life.

The wife never came up, but he did say one thing about keeping promises. He said he respected me for actually leaving town. He recalled the vow I had made about going to Africa. "You left the town, the state, hell, you left the whole country. I envied you for some time, but then I realized I was never going to leave, that I had to stay. Don't think poorly of me, son, but I was doomed to stay here."

"Why?"

"I had to keep remembering. It was the only thing for me."

We went outside and it was a clear night and underneath our stars we built a fire and got his dogs around us and kept after the bottles. He asked me to tell him about Africa and so I did. His face drooped on the flickering glow as he sipped a glass and petted his dogs, their heavy breathing like other voices.

My Zulu girlfriend living in a cave with monkeys appeared. Her black body glistened in the firelight. He asked me what it was like to be with an African woman and I told him this one was pretty rough in bed, but I got used to it. I hesitated, but then out came the German male nurse who had knowingly infected refugees with HIV and how we had thought about having him killed, but didn't. He said that we should have done it to a guy like that, "He deserved killing." I also told him about my buddy, the ex-French Legionnaire going mad and how on some roads in Africa the piles of old clothes you passed would sometimes turn out to be heaps of bodies. There was Rwanda during the slaughter and Somalia during the famines and Sudan during the wars. I told him about the English counsel who would drop his wife off at my house so he could go whoring, the Hutus that I turned over to the Tutsi army, pregnant Emma killed, maybe assassinated, Jade losing her leg in an airdrop, Victor stealing thousands under my nose, the landmines, the malaria, and the dying babies and finally, there were the corpses dropped into gaping lava cracks with bags of quick lime dumped after them and me looking down watching the flies fight and win.

I told him how there was not much to compare to three or four hundred bodies rotting in a hole while thousands of maggots and flies feasted upon the putrid flesh.

After a few hours I started to lose him. It was sort of like going to a bunch of museums or ancient cities one after the other. The paintings and pyramids start to look the same. He stayed awake through it all and was polite and asked questions, but overall he seemed more interested in the fact that I was there, by the fire actually talking to him after all these years. I could have been telling him about crop prices. I don't think it would have mattered.

When we had finished the bottles, I said goodnight and that it was great to see him again. We shook hands with the dawn hinting at the woods. I left all of his dogs sleeping as I started to retrace my journey.

My coach and his wife; they had affected me in different ways. I liked the old man and he had taught me a lesson or two, but his wife meant more.

I thought that of all the death I had known, his wife was the first one that had truly stayed with me. Others before her had only been passing through. She had built a house with a strong frame in my subconscious and roamed around waiting for me to come and give her the due she deserved. I guess that was the real purpose of finding my coach.

Now that I was remembering, she had always been there in the doorway of her house, gently swinging like the pendulum of an old clock. I could finally see her clearly in my mind and then I watched her movement on the end of the rope and I realized that she was taking my measure, counting the seconds of my life as I drove home.

The drink was inside of him like a roaring river. He stood in front of the refugee shacks made of tin and cardboard and bits of plastic. A few were tents. Every time he threw a rock you could hear it shred something and clang into the corrugated metal. He wore a Halloween mask. Come out you motherfuckers! he yelled. I'll fucking kill all you bastards! The refugees knew all about the wrath of the old gods. The hockey mask came to them through the ages. It was near midnight and the rain started. He stood there getting crushed by the African storm that had swept down from the mountains onto the high desert. He shook his fist at different phantoms illuminated by the lightning. Finally, he went back to his tent and passed out. He was an American and the coordinator for refugee housing. Building was his trade and he could do anything you needed done. Plain speaking came to him naturally like the voice of his father telling him to get up so he could hit him again. He was small then and scared and cried easily. He carried the pain around like some of us use backpacks to go shopping.

Of course, none of that American horror story was on the two pages of his highly polished resume when I had hired him. He only brought it to my attention during a shit storm on the Ethiopian border and although his experience had been hard won, it was unfortunately too dark for his technical position.

CENTRAL AFRICAN EMPIRE

THE HEAT NOVEL

THE ELECTRIC ANIMAL DOCTOR stood at the open window of his office looking upon a dying vista. If you had not known him, you might have thought he was having a heart attack, but he was in perfect health and he had a great tan.

To many he was a god.

The day had been long for the Electric Animal Doctor. Temperatures were above 100 degrees and the next month was predicted to be hotter. The wobbly planet was in the midst of a pollution heat wave that among other things had caused birds to fall from the sky, dogs to spin in anguish, fish to fillet themselves, and 650 million butterflies to die in heaps like melted paintings scattered about the landscape.

He wondered who was counting the butterflies; someone from his Ministry or maybe the Food Ministry. He had heard that the butterflies were to be put into squeezable tubes and sold under the brand name "Rainbow Mustard".

The butterflies had died over a chaotic week and he could still feel the movement of their frantic wings as they dropped from the sky and madly tried to hang onto his body. As he looked down at the trail, he watched the naked men driving the gray white donkeys loaded with overflowing sacks of crushed wings.

The dust from the train stirred into the sky drifting toward open throats. Dust for butterflies came into his mind. He like the thought and jotted it down upon microscopic blood tissue.

Heat had become a long historical novel for him with dry, yellowed pages and mad characters that climbed steep steps to the tops of pyramids. He wrote with invisible fingers in his mind. The unseen book was titled, "The Heat Novel".

The words appeared like liquid apparitions upon the cells of his brain. After drying, they were pressed upon sheets of heat. His internal voice had taken the dual roles of critic and publisher. His memory acted as the ultimate library; the final complex of his work as it stacked page after page, pushing toward the sun.

The book was filled with ancient secrets, which were total bullshit, but still, somehow, controlled the lives of people. They were the kind of enigmas that led husbands to kill wives and strangers to drop bombs upon other strangers and priests to abuse children.

His characters performed veiled, meaningless rituals. Humiliation was a momentary, but constant theme. People ended up mostly unhappy and often exploited. Death was not necessarily a friend.

The story played out before an audience of solid air shapes that wore masks. Every drop of sweat on his brow sold the literary value of "The Heat Novel". Skeptics had no place in his developing vision blurred into fractured images by salt.

As he stood watching the donkeys shuffle along to the cries of the naked natives, he was aware of no wind and the sound of people arguing out of open windows. He heard the Minister shouting down the hall. "Never again! Never again!"

One of the Minister's prostitutes was late and he was screaming at a policeman who had been unable to find her in the park. She was a real beauty and all the staff got out of her way when she entered the building. Her hips were dangerous. In twenty minutes she earned what most of them made in a month.

The Minister, of course, was quite right to be upset. When things were at an end, like they were now, quick pleasures were important. Everyone was searching for something to take their minds off the heat and the general downward spiral of things.

People feared the Minister. He was a bastard and he could have most anybody killed for any reason. The killing did not extend to the bigger bastards that he relied upon for his power. He only dreamed about killing them. They were family members and old friends who controlled the system. In a way, he was just playing at being a bastard in comparison to them.

The Electric Animal Doctor had heard the groans of the Minister and the prostitute having sex on the big desk a few days earlier. At least he thought they were on the desk, since the expensive carpet was bloody and no one would want to make love on blood stains. Their automated pleasure had sounded like the echo of a murder.

Torture was one of the policies that seemed to work in this country. People responded to it and things moved along unexpectedly like paper dancing in the street. When he first noticed the pink and maroon splotches of oxidized gore on the carpet he had thought nothing of it, other than the cleaning staff was probably in trouble.

Everywhere there were horrible things to contemplate and eventually they grew large in his mind and ended up harassing him. Sleep was chained to a tree just outside his window at home and late at night he could hear it rustling about in the decay.

The last time he had gone into the Minister's office was to drop off an egg market report. The Minister was interested in eggs, although he never ate them. He was irritated by eggs. He didn't like the way the yoke broke so easily and ran across the plate losing its heat before he could actually sop it up.

For the Minister, eggs were an inferior food. He liked meat; particularly the buttocks of young girls, breaded in corn meal and fried with garlic and chili. Those sorts of meals soothed him like the gentle stroking of his favorite aunt's hand on his thigh.

Eggs for the Minister meant money. He and the Royal Family owned most of the large layer plants. He counted on the Electric Animal Doctor to give him supply and demand reports from time to time. Capitalism to the Minister, however, was more of an invitation than an economic theory.

The electricity had gone out two days earlier, paralyzing the gears of the Electric Animal Doctor's oscillating floor fan. The smooth, dust free fan was new and he had found it on the black market and paid for it himself. It was one of the few things he liked in the office.

No one else in the building had one, so when the heat started in earnest, anonymous staff suddenly became friendly. They found reasons to stand near his desk and ask absurd questions. He didn't mind. The aimless talk brightened his day and he enjoyed watching the ridiculous words flutter about the room like virtual wings beating time to his initiative and motor.

In the midst of all that coolness he felt validated, better than everyone else. In fact the whole scene made him feel human, but not magnificent; that only came when he knelt as a god and cold as death beside his animals.

The large clock in the foyer finally touched five and people rushed out of the Ministry building. He decided to wait in his office and run his fan. The electricity was out, but that wouldn't stop him. The night watchman was old and usually never came to his floor, so he knew he could electrify undisturbed.

He unplugged the fan's cord from the wall socket. The fan had a three pronged plug. From his desk he retrieved a thick rubber band and wrapped it around the plug. Next he looped the rubber band around his ear. The plug hung down his head just beside his ear canal. It didn't have to be too tight against his head in order to work. He only needed to expose the metal prongs to the ear canal.

The fan slowly began to turn. Electricity was transferring from his body through the prongs and wiring in the cord and into the motor of the fan. He leaned back and enjoyed the cool wind upon his face. Slowly he began to lose body heat and after about five minutes he pulled the plug away from his ear and the fan stopped. He didn't want to consume too much of his electricity because the animals might come tonight.

When he finally left the building the sun had dropped far below the crest of mountains surrounding the city. The temperature was still above 100 degrees. Only the moon provided light.

The route home was always the same. He walked through the long, jagged canyon where thousands of years before an ocean of lava had rushed down the sides of young volcanoes. Boulders, the size of houses, lay about like state-sponsored art. They often hid thieves with short knives and long green sticks cut from the few remaining trees near the river. But he didn't mind the danger. He hardly thought about it, even when a few of the locals had been killed on the same path.

Rumor had it that the victims were rendered for their organs. He laughed at that. Who would want his heart or brain? His dick and balls were worthless; maybe his eyes were of some value, the ones that continued to see even when the lids were closed. But whatever they took from his sliced pile, he felt certain they would be disappointed. The joke would be on them; the witch doctors and the cannibals and the teachers from the agricultural school. They would bag him by the kilogram and sell him as an import, but in the end the quality would not be there. His taste and texture amounted to the worst sort of fraud. Surely the butchers along his way home could recognize that.

When he walked through his front door he immediately noticed there was no smell of food in the air. Elizabeth had not cooked. Strange he thought, she always had his food ready. He dropped his bag and made his way to the bedroom, leaving his clothes behind on the floor.

As he lay naked on the bed he began to write "The Heat Novel" in his mind. The warmth in his room was an inspiration. He watched as the heat fell in transparent sheets, layer upon layer across the room. The words floated out of his mind and graved the thin heat pages; moving, alive, falling into place, and building toward the climactic end which he was still figuring out.

Surely people would like his work; maybe in other times, other places. Fame and bank accounts came to him as he stood among smiling faces, but then he asked a question that completely stopped his writing: Was it possible to drown in heat? Panicked he asked another. Could heat burn all the oxygen out of the air and produce a combustible gas that would fill lungs until they exploded in a burst of flame? If he had been a slave in the hold of a ship perhaps he would know. He began to fixate on burning up from the inside, wondering how a fire might be able to start in an organ or a limb.

He decided to have a drink. There was a gin bottle on his bedside table.

A photograph of an old lover looked down upon him from a cracked mirror. The bending snapshot showed a strong sexual intensity in her eyes: her black shadow was elongated by a low sun and far in the distance a truck was just cresting a little hill on an asphalt highway. He looked at it and vaguely recalled the feeling of entering her body on the grass of a ruin. But that was another time, when he had a normal name and a semblance of lucidity. Had they been hitchhiking? Did he have a car? He couldn't remember.

He was the Electric Animal Doctor now and his old life was as useless as somebody else's memories at the moment of their death. He had decided to live alone, to be alone, and to only wear blank expressions. This meant most of his dreams were lost when he awoke in the morning.

There was no one there sharing his pillow; no one to tell about being terrified in dark halls or floating on the sea or taking tests or having sex with inappropriate people. Funny, he had once been a dreamer and now he was without dreams. They left him each morning within a few seconds of gaining consciousness.

He rose and passed through the sheer gauze curtains that led to the balcony. The air was still and he thought he heard the distant sounds of animals. He mixed himself a warm gin and tonic, sat down, and put his feet up on the rail that kept him from tumbling into the garden when he was drunk.

The laugh of a woman came from below. Still naked, he walked down the path beside his house. A dark human form was lying on the ground. It was Elizabeth. She was stoned from having spooned too much marijuana soup. He took her by the hand and led her to the gate. Her blouse was open and she was bare foot and there was a handkerchief tied around her head.

"No food tonight," she giggled. "Okay, maybe tomorrow?"

He hugged her upward and she lifted slightly off the ground. "Goodnight," she smiled with perfect white teeth that shone in the moonlight and then she turned and disappeared into the darkness. "Tomorrow," he whispered after her and then he slowly returned to the balcony.

The gin filled his veins and he looked hard into the night. A pair of sunglasses and a ball of copper wire were on the table beside him.

He wondered if they would come. Sometimes he had to wait for days; but then it happened. The first animal to stop in the bushes was a fox and then quickly a wild dog, a goat, a leopard, a blackbird, and a rabbit. A snake was also there, but it had come only to see what was going on. They all lay in a little group upon a flat strip of ground near a low row of hedges. Their eyes glowed like tail lights as they looked toward him.

The Electric Animal Doctor picked up the copper wire and put on the sunglasses and went to them through the hot air with a smile on his face.

They gathered around him as he lay down upon the grass. He became like shallow water and within a few minutes more animals silently placed their bodies near him.

Soon there were thirty or so animals; they were with and without fur, a few birds, many with hooves, two footed, four footed, paws, claws, and some with thick hides. They moaned and grunted and breathed in unhealthy wheezes that sounded like old women praying. Save the snake, they were all warm blooded.

They had dropped their instincts to come to him there in the garden. Naked he felt as one with them. The creatures closest to him licked his skin. He became aroused. The sweat from his body cooled them and it dissipated upon the roughness of their tongues.

They were all innocent and gentle on the grass as if in a religious painting out of a thick book that no one read anymore. The ritual called for one animal to be sacrificed. He didn't know how they settled upon the one to die. Perhaps by age or disposition or size; he really didn't want to know and then a young bear nudged forward across the grass and put its head directly next to his.

He slipped the copper wire between their heads and began to force his electricity into the head of the bear. Twenty minutes passed and then the bear's body began to singe and little fires erupted in the fur and within a few more minutes it was dead, smoking in the grass.

A lion drug it into the bush and quickly returned.

His body temperature had fallen dangerously low, but that was the point. He was a god for the animals and they drew their heads closer to him and nuzzled his form. They were as polite as hot animals could be and his coldness ran into their noses and faces and feathers and skin and they licked and brushed and slid over him again and again until they began to cool down.

They all knew him as the Electric Animal Doctor. The recognition ran deep in their brains like moon lit shadows giving life to animal drawings on the walls of ancient, damp caves.

They stayed this way for the rest of the night, intermittently touching each other with a coolness that others could never know as the planet became hotter and hotter. Just before dawn they began to leave him and the last to go was a wild dog. He watched it disappear in the hedge as the light slowly turned up in the early morning.

With his sunglasses on the sun rose and he lay naked in the grass absorbing the solar waves like a movie star on a hidden beach far from the crowds that worshipped him. The sun replenished his electricity and his tan changed into even more gorgeous shades of gold.

After an hour or two, he got up and went into the house. He drew a bath to remove the smell of the animals and began to get ready for his work day. He wondered how long any of this would last? He supposed that it really didn't matter. He was resigned to the death of the planet; his death.

He was committed to living alone, without dreams, without a future, but still there was a dark irritation that lingered in his spirit. It had to do with the animals and their helplessness. That was something he occasionally felt very acutely, particularly now as he closed the front door and headed toward the Ministry carrying in his bag an unedited report on the revenue potential of palm oil.

I am home now and time allows me to look into the distance with a knowing, blank expression. All the beer and mezcal that I want is available. I think about what I am seeing. Don't others understand what is happening? The world is melting and the misery plays out before me like a wounded dog thrashing around on the highway. Maybe there is something wrong with me. During the hot evenings, I walk through my All-American community searching for someone with my eyes. After a while I am depressed and then the fear starts. Inside the houses, people rot on plastic furniture while they slap their bellies with vile comfort. I can see them through the windows in the dark. Their eyes are like black flies and they send them outside to attack me. Grumpy teachers and government officials stand around watching in approval and a few start to fill out papers on me. Their eyes are on fire. In a burst of panic I fall face down upon somebody's lawn. The bottles of beer I am holding break and cut my hands. Blood leaks out of me. I lay there for a while in the moonlight. I am exhausted, but not totally nuts. Not yet anyway. I need a few more years of taking toxic medicines before my illness evolves into something more lethal. In the end, even my dogs will be unsure, but yet, they will follow me into the alley. The blood keeps flowing onto the grass and the stars fade away. This is how it is in a world without enough eyes that can see.

GUATEMALA

TORTILLA MOUTH

I STOPPED IN FRONT of my favorite tortillaria. Hunger was pawing my stomach like a trapped rat. The rapid sound of my girlfriend's clicking shoes was right behind me.

The girl and I had been arguing all night. The scab was just hardening on the side of my face where she had caught me with her high heel. After attacking me, she started crying and asked me to hit her, so I did.

People dodged us on the sidewalk. Her voice was loud, irrational, but with dramatically timed pauses. She stood with the back of her right hand underneath her left elbow as the left arm extended out in front of her like a nurse was about to draw blood from her vein. She bit her lip as she flicked ashes off her cigarette, expecting the usual end to our quarrels.

Sex was our disease. Hot, quick breathing ignited sick fires inside our bodies. I could smell her even though we were standing in the middle of Guatemala City. Her scent held up pleasantly against the bus exhaust and piss on the walls.

Growing up with violence and death squads had given her super powers and she was used to having her way with men. Life for her was tentative and she was emotionally unbalanced. Her family was rich and politically cross-connected. Masked men had kidnapped and killed her father.

The government blamed the communists, but the mother thought the right-wing repression of "White Hand" was to blame. No one ever asked for a ransom and they had found his body in a hole behind a Mexican restaurant with a view.

One night after three quarters bottle of inflammable Tick Tack and lime, she casually mentioned how her father had abused her. It had been a secret between them.

She told her story in monochrome like an old black and white photo chemically deteriorating in front of my eyes. The father had eventually felt guilty and sent her out of the country. Living with relatives in Florida, she earned a degree from the University of Miami. She won beauty contests and got a job on television.

Her relations with men were chaotic and fierce. She kept saying she needed me to change her life. On the surface of her retina were the reflections of a bunch of broken guys in handcuffs. I noticed them the first time we made love and that had always worried me.

She was a woman itching to commit a desperate act. I figured she had it in her to cut my throat some night when I was passed out. She would justify it for something I had said; nothing major, just words that would run like a wild beast through her heart and down to her hand, the one that held the knife.

She was shadowy in that way and I often imagined her walking naked down the hallway to where I lay sleeping like the tolling of a bell.

We looked at each other. The tips of her red fingernails extended toward me. She wanted me to take her hand so she could lead me back to her place. I knew I wouldn't be able to resist her soft walls. We would have angry sex and my dick would be like a hammer. We would rebuild new, crazy days for her to throw things, threaten and scream.

I had learned a lot living with her. I came to understand how people were able to equate love with pain.

Our scars, her little daughter's scars, were visible for those interested enough to see.

I turned away and went into the tortillaria. The simple movement of my body was like a eulogy in the doorway. She stood alone, the last mourner at my grave. I got to the counter and asked for a half kilo of tortillas.

"Fuck your tortillas," she said.

When I looked back over my shoulder, she was gone. I would never see her again.

A young girl wrapped my order in wax paper and then dropped it into a clear plastic sack and gave it a twist. I stepped onto the sidewalk where my lover had just been. I placed the tortillas up against my face and the heat radiated into my cheek. Replacing her strange emotion with the warmth of food seemed like a good choice and I stood there for a moment lost in my nuzzling.

My leather bag hung over my shoulder and I placed the food inside. As I walked I decided to eat a tortilla. The plastic sack that held them was in the bottom of my bag. I managed to get one hand around the pile and started to move the paper out of the way so I could peel one off to eat.

As I fumbled with the wrapping, a man stepped onto the sidewalk in front of me. He was exiting a luxury hotel.

He was dressed impeccably. His suit was way out of place on the grubby streets of Guatemala City. Behind him emerged two other men, also in shiny suits. Bringing up the rear were two policemen carrying snub nosed machine pistols. They cradled them like newborns. I thought about stopping, but instead I kept fiddling with my tortilla.

Finally, I recognized the face of the first man. He was in charge of a large portfolio in the state security apparatus and had been instrumental in fabricating the façade of peace talks. Ronald Reagan was his favorite person on the planet and he had a reputation for harsh, lethal discrimination toward indigenous people.

Simple politics were below him. The inner circle was his office and where he presided, disappearances, torture, and death soon followed. In the glance of his eyes I saw no leniency, no second chances. As he approached I felt sorry for everyone who had stood or knelt in front of him and I could see their withering bodies and painful resignation.

They were the doomed of Guatemala.

When I was about ten feet from the group I finally managed to get a single tortilla into my hand. A problem still existed. The other tortillas would all fall out in my bag unless I twisted the top of the sack closed. For that trick I needed both hands. My only alternative was to place the tortilla in my mouth, thereby freeing my hands to twist the sack closed.

Just at that moment I looked up at the state security boss. We were perhaps five feet apart. Our eyes met and he saw the tortilla hanging from my mouth covering my chin. My hands were just twisting the plastic sack closed inside my bag. His lips pressed into a slight smile. One of the men to his side began to reach for my bag. The policemen also started to move.

The man who was used to condemning people barked a command and everyone froze in place. He stopped and I stopped. He pointed to the tortilla and laughed and told the two men in suits that this was the funniest thing he had seen in months.

He seemed like a normal human being at that moment and I felt a wave of disdain for this man who was a close ally of my country. When he extended his hand to press my arm I saw a light rose colored stain on his skin.

All of his men started laughing and then they got into three black SUVs and drove away, leaving me standing there with the tortilla in my mouth.

A few seconds later as I walked and ate my tortilla in the hot sun of Guatemala City I considered the importance of what had just happened. Tortillas, the life giver, had brought us all together. I decided that I would never eat another one again without recalling my abused, violent lover and the laughing killer and the taste of ground corn on my tongue would be like a secret wafer for the battered and damned of Guatemala.

I was lucky. My contract was over. I was going home to see my dying father and wondered if the god that I knew was not there might find it in his absent, empty heart to allow my father to leave this world without too much more pain.

My new goal was to find a decent hotel room for a few days. Get away from the uncommon girl; some place with a quiet bar. Along about midnight I'd be drunk. Abnormal thoughts would come to me and I'd stumble out into the streets, dodging women with open purses that advertised hand lotion. A place in the shadows would find me and I'd watch the night people being picked up and thrown into vans driven by men in civilian clothes saluting each other.

The kid was an RPG casualty. How he had survived was anybody's guess. I took the end of the stretcher and looked down at the small shape in the darkness. His bones smiled at me. It was hard to tell, what with the black soot and blood covering his body, but he looked about four years old. He was in shock and I had come to understand that there was a certain type of child who was able to escape from trauma and journey to a spot without pain. Along the way they'd bless those who hurt them, forgive strangers for unknown sins. The final destination was a serene, trouble-free hotel—every kid with the right stuff knew the place and as I looked down at the little head tipping from side to side, I could tell this one was already checked into his room.

THE SUDAN

HALF A BLACKBIRD

I HAVE BEEN LIVING inside Teresa's ear for almost ten years now. Her acoustics allow me to say what I want, be who I am. She will always be young to me, since our birthdates are separated by a lot of living. The more my eyesight fails the better she looks. Her beautiful face is accepting of my stories like the friendly greeter at a nightclub opening the door for me and my highflying friends.

Love is working out for me.

Like many people in a marriage, I have not been totally honest with her. Sometimes I have to leave her and go far away. It is hard for me to control. I am trying to make it better, but it is difficult.

We have come to the store. I wait in the car as she walks away. She turns and mouths "Merry Christmas" as she disappears through the electric doors into a hidden world of boxes and foreign languages that mask evil with fine print. Few think about the pain that buying inexpensive crap made by children and slaves can cause. Cheap gizmos seem like good deals until you start to look closely at the solder or stitching and find pleas for help written in very tiny letters by prisoners and suicidal workers.

I switch on the radio and turn up the volume. A grizzled Santa Claus from Oklahoma smokes a cigarette beside a sign that says, "Everything Must Go! Are you ready?" He looks at me intently as if to say that things aren't quite as merry as his suit implies.

Maybe he takes a step toward me. Is he coming my way? I don't know, because I'm already leaving. The only question is where?

The Santa Claus has a face like someone has stolen Christmas. I take his look as my escort and I am arrested by the law of falling bodies.

Roaring wind Africanizes my heart and my eyes are shot with lions.

Africa comes to me on spools.

The Antonov 24 makes a slow approach over the little town of Kapoeta in southern Sudan. The Russian pilot speaks through his head set to one of his crewmen who signals to the Arabs in the cargo hold to start pushing the eight FAB-250 kilogram bombs toward the tail end of the big plane.

They fall gracefully with no apparent target other than the outline of the town below.

I extend my hand into a long stripe of African history.

As the bombs drop high overhead, Ba slowly becomes disturbed as he reads a week old newspaper. Shirtless in shorts and flip flops, he sits on a canvas camp chair, the kind Hemingway and Roosevelt used when safaris were really unsafe and mostly stupid.

Ba looks up from the newspaper, he eyes a group of Sudanese workers and soldiers resting under a few thorny shittah trees. Unable to contain himself, he shouts: "Captain, mobilize your men! They are idle, doing nothing!"

At that moment, he hears the sound of the airplane, but it doesn't immediately register with him since the airstrip is fairly close to the camp. He is used to the noise of incoming relief flights. But then the engines get louder and he hears whistles like panicked nights and he vaguely recalls his time in Laos. He knows the sound of falling bombs.

Ba is an official observer for the U.N. and is also a refugee from Burma. He escaped over the border into Laos many years ago and can't go back. He carries Burma around with him in a sack that he sometimes opens to allow the cool fog from the Lake of No Return to undulate across his naked body.

Spiders crawling along the mosquito net watch him sleep under a cover of white mist. They figure in their own spider way that he is different, perhaps a god from a lost land.

The first bombs hit near the hospital, as they always seem to, and then move toward the camp. The Dinka, donkeys, goats, and cattle run wildly as if both man and beast are chasing chickens. Five naked Taposa tribesmen stand around making shadows like pencil drawings. It is hard to get them excited, but after a few seconds they squat, sliding down their walking sticks as they take their height closer to the ground.

Ba sprints into his own personal trench. It is dark as he stoops and stumbles along the bottom. He is afraid of black mambas, but the bombs make him forget about the one that slithered out a few weeks ago.

His imagination is more focused upon the possibility that one of the bombs is headed directly for the top of his head. He has been thinking lately that there is an X on his bald spot, the kind that cartoon characters are always drawing on things they want to destroy.

The job in the Sudan had not been his first choice. He wanted to go to Haiti to work on a U.N. project that was attempting to track the sale of human body parts. Baby Doc Duvalier was apparently making money on shipments of unauthorized vital organs.

Ba had schmoozed an older, well-preserved female New York staffer and thought the job was his. Unfortunately, his cocktail lounge interviews hadn't worked out, so here he was in a snake infested hole listening to bombs explode.

He still held out hope that he would get a call from her.

"She owe me," he'd say. "And it be pretty easy to trace body parts. Don't you think?"

"I don't know. Where would you start?"

"Follow doctors. That's where to begin. She's talking about office in Miami. Chase the bikinis too. Good R&R!"

"I see," I said. "You'd sort of expand your search for body parts to include the girls on the beach."

"That's right. Why not?" he laughed.

The dream job never materialized. The stolen body parts would continue to travel without his well-paid concern and the beach girls never got to show him their wild parts either.

As a substitute for all that, he decided to become a pain in the collective ass of the Sudan People's Liberation Army. He cussed and argued with the military types and broke all their local bullshit rules. He was particularly interested in child soldiers. I'd tell him to relax. Surprise visits to controlled areas were not necessarily the best way to work, but he had been in too many tough spots to really care what anyone thought about him.

Eight people were killed that day in the Antonov bombing attack, an insignificant amount for Africa, where every white death is worth ten thousand black deaths in the world's press. Ba survived to write a long report to his superiors. But, as we all do, he eventually ended up dead. His fate came at the bottom of a rocky ravine along the Uganda border.

It went something like this: Ba sits in the front passenger seat of a Toyota SUV. A Kenyan is driving. In the back sit a Thai nurse and a Swedish journalist. Ba is criticizing the holes in the road quietly to the driver just as they come around a sharp turn and run into a group of soldiers firing at a lineup of their so-called enemies.

The vehicle stops right in front of the bodies. There is a few seconds of that smoky, frozen, ringing silence which follows the blast of guns and then the lone voice of a commander rises up and orders his troops to fire on the vehicle. It is a split second command decision reflecting conditions on the ground and unavoidable in the context of the mad war.

That's what they say anyway.

Ba, being the great athlete he is, jumps out and runs down into a large hole that has been eroded by a flash flood. He is chased by a 14-year old with an AK-47, who recently climbed down from the sky on a rope. When Ba trips, the kid gives one of those sweeping, can't miss type of shots that rips Ba's back open and dislodges some of the body parts that he wanted to track down so badly.

At that precise moment a blue bird appears and cuts the line that tethers Ba to the earth and then he is no more.

Back at the vehicle, both the driver and the journalist are sitting dead. The female nurse is wounded and becomes invisible on the floorboard. After a short discussion they stitch her up. Somebody does a nice job.

Later she finds herself on a cot near a fire in the desert and they inject her with some sort of drug. Three days later she awakes to the gentle motion of them placing a blindfold on her eyes and then they lead her to a spreading green bush and one of them steps forward and shoots her in the head.

Santa weaves in and out of the air that surrounds my life. I hear music. The Santa is hanging on my window now speaking to me in that weather beaten Oklahoma accent that gets people nowhere.

Like an unread poem I am lifeless, but then I hear Nilsson's song "Without Her". The Santa is wondering about me, but somehow seems impressed.

"I haven't heard Nilsson in years," he says. "You like that guy? It brings back a lot of memories." Without waiting for me to answer he turns away and disappears.

Suddenly, Teresa is there. She's been gone about five minutes. I am embarrassed to tell her where I have been. My past is always taking over my present and I am afraid it will be making a move on my future soon. The old days seem to be armed and are looking to cover all of my time in a white sheet.

"Did you find the part for the faucet?" I look at her sideways.

She shakes her head no. "Just waiting?" she asks.

"Yeah, I'm just waiting for you, listening to Nilsson."

I glance at the empty parking spaces in front of me. The eight dead Sudanese from the bombing run, the journalist, the driver, and the nurse are all stretched out in a line. Humanitarians place groups of dead people in lines; the other bastards just pile them up.

Ba's mangled body is propped up against a stray shopping cart. Blood forms in a circle around him. Taken as a whole they look like photographic evidence of war crimes for some prosecutor in the Hague. Right, that's not going to happen.

"It looked like you were talking to the Santa Claus," Teresa says.

"Not really."

As I pull out onto the street, I know what the drivers are thinking, what happened here years ago, why the trees are dying, and who will finally knock on my door with the bad news.

My body breaks into pieces and drifts down the highway trying to keep up with the car I am driving; caught on the wind, each part revolves in space trying to come together like a swirling circle of blackbirds that wheel and fall, faster and faster, into half of their name: the dark, mysterious half, the one that shrouds my form.

We are all self-haters, particularly at 2:00 a.m. or so. In those moments when we shake off a dream, lie detection is acute. The reckoning comes with clammy skin and staring straight up at the dark ceiling where the bugs crawl. A clock ticks like a guilty verdict. Exiled mistakes return as carpenters who rebuild memories we are trying to forget: angry enemies, screwed innocents, disappointed friends and family, those shunned or hurt in a hundred secret ways that only we know about. There are little children we abused and neglected or partners we cheated or friends we ruined or lovers we destroyed.

People we left for dead. The nights are dark for a reason. Dealing with bad memories is not just restricted to waking from a nightmare. Part of the curse is falling. I am a big faller. From a great height I drop down into old memories, tumbling out of control. It can come anytime, anywhere. I can fall in bed or driving a car or talking to a very important person. There is usually an internal bolt of electricity that deletes my outward bodily expression. A few seconds of the surge causes everything to go white, as if I have taken a shot to the head and then geometric patterns move across the surface of my eyes. I start falling then, but sometimes I can fake it and continue being there, but only with that faraway look that connects my eyes to something in the distance. My answers to questions are delayed. Conversations are strange. I pick up only the tail end of sentences and make off topic comments. People often think I am rude, but the truth is I am falling. That is the way of my world. That is the way I wake in the night and that is the way I fall. I wonder if others are like me.

HONDURAS

MY INSIGNIFICANT RELATIONSHIP WITH STARS

REFUGEES HAVE ALWAYS BEEN trudging along the roads in front of my houses, laying down cardboard in the empty lots of my life. They inched their way out of the pages of National Geographic and World Book when I was a kid. I can still see their weathered faces on those shiny clean pages, hoping that a reader somewhere would take them out of the photo and build them a fire and feed them a cracked cup of soup.

I got in a fight over refugees in high school. I gave a report on the Spanish Civil War, when the stars began to fly across the sky and drop bombs on the unsuspecting sheep herders and black haired lovers of the Basque country.

I brought a bota wine bag some sheep had reluctantly given up its stomach for. I demonstrated how to drink wine from its black spout. Orange juice dribbled down my chin.

My father had the bag out in our garage, stuck on a dark, dusty shelf lined with empty oil filters. It was brittle and smelly and sewn together with red twine. I figured it would make an exciting opening for my library research about the Spanish Civil War.

I told my class about Madrid, Guernica, and Bilbao and how Hitler had decided to do a bit of practice fighting in Spain, allowing his air force to execute indiscriminate carpet bombing in 1937.

He wanted to take the fight out of the Republican army by dropping bombs on their wives, children and grandmothers. Imagining the twisted bodies of burned civilians must have brought a crooked smile to his face. Killing families instead of troops came to Hitler like finding expensive candy inside a rotting piece of meat.

The Reader's Digest called it "terror bombing". It was the first time anyone had used that phrase. As I spoke about this exotic, unknown war that gave birth to things that would ultimately control our lives, most of the girls in class were mesmerized, their eyeballs frozen and floating in a large glass lab jar on a nearby metal table.

But the boys didn't think too much of what I was saying. They seemed nervous like poisonous snakes were hanging over their heads.

I described how about 25,000 Basque children from Bilbao were sent out of the country to escape the Fascist bombs. They were the largest group of refugee children the world had ever taken notice of. Places like England and Mexico took them in, but America refused. The American Catholic Church objected to helping the children of communists.

Practiced looks came from a guy named Joe. He had a set of expressions like boxers give to mirrors or the insane to cupped hands. More than just a mean face, it was a life in the balance, as if everything depended upon those looks.

After class he went home and scheduled an ambush for the next morning over the phone with his friends. I got wind of the planned attack and early the next day I went by my friend Willy's house. He was the quarterback and I was the end. It was about 6:00 a.m. He rolled over and looked at me through the window screen.

I asked if he would like to accompany me to the massacre. He said no, today was not my "lucky star." At the time I thought it was an odd answer.

So I walked away from his house that used to be a post office, alone and with nothing ahead of me except what my father would later call "a good lesson."

As I approached the school parking lot, Joe leaned against a car with ten or so of his friends in a semi-circle around him. Some of them were at least 21 years old and wore the kind of leather jackets that said in menacing, highly tanned tones that they were waiting for me and all my Basque bull shit stories.

They looked like terror bombers getting ready to unload.

After it was over I had a fractured jaw, a cut eye, and bloody knuckles. I made it to class anyway and when I saw Joe in the hall I ran him down and tackled him at the top of a flight of stairs. We ended up in a heap and he came out of it with a broken arm.

Joe was unable to live out a full life of wife beating, heavy drinking, and being late, because when he got old enough to buy his own leather jacket he made a comment to a black man about the black man's white wife and the black man pulled a knife and cut one of Joe's arteries. He bled to death on the concrete slab of a heavily neon lit hamburger stand; the kind with a slanted tin roof and speakers where you can order from your car and feel like somebody special for $1.99.

The grand jury, in a notoriously redneck county and despite the best efforts of the god-appointed good old boy prosecutor, decided to no-bill the black man. It was front page news. The exact thing Joe had said to the black man was never made public.

Years later I worked in La Mosquitia, Honduras with 25,000 Mosquito Indian refugees. I had a Basque lover and Bilbao was her hometown.

Maritxu was a doctor and had wide Basque feet and a beautiful head of black hair. She had the kind of beauty that was put there by the illumination of candles from the dark of a burned out building. Her eyes were like the aftermath of a bombing run and when she stared at me I felt as if I were injured.

During sex she dug her fingernails into my back. Some of the divots and scratches got infected and once I came down with a fever. I didn't mind so much and never really felt her nails until later when I took a bath and washed with soap.

Maritxu was also a non-stop smoker. I had watched my father waste away with the killing effects of cigarettes, so while getting my back turned into hamburger didn't bother me, a lover who chain smoked did.

I went on a hunger strike and told her that as long as she smoked, I wouldn't eat. She was greatly impressed with my imitation of Gandhi and stopped smoking. She took my vow not to eat as a sign of love, but after a few days love gave way to nicotine addiction.

At night I would watch her hide in the shadows by the river and set her face on fire.

She had strong communist views. I could support that, but her brother was a member of ETA, the Basque separatist group that liked to blow up streets in Madrid that might have important Spanish politicians on them. He was in a maximum security prison back in Spain. She told me how they tortured her to get at him.

The white scars were raised on the inside of her thighs and just below the hollow of her back was a deep, round burn mark. My fingers always tried to avoid her haunted ground. She never cried and was hard in that way, but her body was soft and feminine, which made for a contemplative mix of elements as we drew closer.

Her past became the wounded lips that I kissed.

We found ourselves naked and uncomfortable in the damp grass huts along the brown Patuca and Coco Rivers. We'd take boat trips into the lagoon. Rain and mosquitoes were our day and night and time passed slowly as the sense-filled jungle grew and moved around us.

The refugees slipped along dappled paths covered with mirrors and black vines joined to snakes. Sometimes the boys and girls lay on the high, dark dry spots and made love. One night a leopard tried to get into our hut. Maritxu took it as a sign of the passion between us. Although I liked the sound of that, I also thought the meat jerky in our food box might have contributed to the poetic incident.

Patrols of Honduran military stopped at our store, PapaBiz. I treated them to fruit juice and candy. Our main business was the exchange of basic jungle supplies, rope, netting, buckets, etc., for the rice and beans the refugees grew.

No money, just barter. It was the old Indian way and everybody was happy.

Soon La Mosquitia was food sufficient, at least in rice and beans, and we saved the U.N. millions on food transport costs.

The icon of PapaBiz was our macaw, Filipe. Stanley found him as a chick in the jungle. He had fallen out of a tree and hurt himself. We nursed him back until he was all grown up and mean as you might expect a slightly lame captive macaw to be.

Stanley was my friend and trusted Indian counterpart. He was a drunk and we first met when I got him out of a hole the Honduran army had thrown him into. It was about six feet deep with a bamboo cover.

We shook hands through the space between the stalks as he reached up to me. He had sort of tried to rape a missionary woman. It was all a big drunken Indian mistake that stretched back a few hundred years.

Stanley loved Filipe. They were a lot alike, both likable, but prone to destruction and poor decisions. When Stanley and I would leave camp, Filipe would get mad and claw his way into our bedrooms and eat our leather belts and crap on our sheets.

One day his clipped feathers had grown back long enough for him to fly. He made a wide circle over the river and lit in a tree on the other side. He stayed there the whole day and then flew back to his little nest in the tree above our line of huts.

He did the same thing for about two weeks and then he was gone, back into the jungle to live like a page from a child's coloring book with other birds and butterflies and happy rainbows. Those were my hopes for him anyway.

Just down the river was MamaBiz, a bar and whorehouse run by a sleazy Honduran trader and gold prospector. He hated me and Stanley and our bird. I never liked him either. He had stolen our name, but I had to give it to him, his basic concept was funny.

He was always trying to sell me a boat full of holes. It looked impressive, but that was all.

"Why would I want a panga ready to sink?" I'd ask.

"You never know," he'd reply. "You might need it someday."

He was shady, no doubt, but I found his sense of humor to be a murky tonic for the weirdness that was the war at our feet.

These were the days of the Sandinistas and the Contra War. It was real enough, but not exactly rampaging. The old conquistadors, spouting poetry and bible verse in the undergrowth, found our efforts mostly pathetic. They were looking for a bit more blood. Bigger productions than rolling hand grenades into discos or kidnapping a few villages and putting them in reeducation camps.

I guess guys like Oliver North were also disappointed. It never became the Vietnam they were hoping for.

One night I was drinking heavily with a Captain in the Honduran Army and I let slip that my Basque lover was from a family that had ETA in its blood. A few weeks later the Honduran Ministry of Interior revoked Maritxu's visa and put her on a plane. I never told her about my drunken conversation: more indications of my weakness.

Eventually I got a letter from her: she had returned to Bilbao, where the children had so long ago escaped the terror bombs and had stumbled off the pages of a book and into my high school history class and then stood around and watched as I got the hell beat out of me.

Maritxu was in prison and had contracted malaria. Someone in the Spanish government had noticed her deportation and had decided to hold her for a few months. They were treating her well and she hoped to be out soon. She wrote that in her dreams we were together in Honduras, floating down the Patuca and that we would look up at the stars and watch them turn into spaceships that gathered us up and beyond this universe and into a happier, long-stretched time.

After that letter, I never heard from the children of Bilbao again, but I have contemplated the meaning of stars more than once in my life and I feel a certain kinship with them in a totally insignificant sort of way, like the last short breath of an ignorant man looking upward into a bank of neon lights or maybe a tortured Basque doctor contracting malaria in the prison of my poor decisions.

I guess small, unknowable things are what we are made of, even more so at the end.

Sometimes letters are long and other times short. Once I got a three page letter with three big words. First page: WHERE, second page: ARE, third page: YOU? I couldn't reply since I was in a bad spot and the only kind of stamps I could get were on fire and the post office had run off with a field hospital from out of town.

HONDURAS/NICARAGUA

PEACE IN THE JUNGLE

THE JUNGLE IS REMOVED from people, but not politics. I don't need to go too far off the trail to be alone in the universe. The big fish jumping, the colorful birds, humidity, concealed snakes, and the vast mud estate are my confidantes.

The jungle can be an inflexible place. A small incline in the dead floor can be lethal and it is difficult to step ahead through broad, tough leaves that hide disaster. Should I fall and be unable to rise, it will be like starring in my own monster movie. The floor is where things die and decompose and if I end up there with a broken leg or a busted head, I won't last long.

I hardly ever see the ground beneath my feet, but I hear it. When I walk, it crunches and squishes and almost always sucks at my boots or flip flops. I have lost many flip flops to the thick mud. The animals live there, stalking around low in the shadows, waiting for my feet to move by and deciding if I am something to eat.

Politics has descended upon this part of the world. All the great powers seem to be interested in the jungle that surrounds me. Most of the Indians are in a state of either panic or depression as conferences, money, and secret negotiations distress their lives like storms raining metal. There is a tribe called the Rama which is undergoing a rash of "Sudden Adult Death Syndrome" or SADS as they say.

Perfectly fit young men go to bed and then wake up dead for no apparent reason. It seems to be caused by a great case of sadness that grips a person's heart and then forces a return into the past for things lost.

For some enigmatic reason, you can only go back in time if you are mostly young, healthy, male, and dead. Belief in the transmutation of the human body helps sadness stop hearts. Parents of the departed sit by the river at night hoping to see the spirits of their children swimming in the water as fish or dolphins lost up river.

A local shaman gives me permission to help the Indians search the moonlit surface of the river. The shaman and I are not exactly friends since he often goes into whirling fits and once smashed into me on the trail, but his approval is necessary. I spend long hours with the families and we usually share a drink or two. Sometimes the Indians point and get excited, but I never see anything except the undulating current flashing silver light.

When I am depressed by the mold, moisture, and dying Indians, I look up and hunt for holes in the tree canopy where the sun can enter. I love jungle trees. They are the steel and turbines of the jungle and they rise with production as if the Industrial Revolution has taken a wrong turn into the Garden of Eden.

Holes let the sun crash into the branches and leaves and land on the black floor. The fragmenting light, flowing through the trees, is the stain glass window of the rainforest and the wispy light hits my face like a sad adagio for strings.

I think I can look upward into the pacific musical opening forever. It is better than gazing out at the impersonal ocean; it is more intimate and lyrical and the warmth is like finding my way home.

Sometimes I disappear into the numbness of the plants.

A few weeks ago, I was quietly resting in the gnarled roots of a large tree and a patrol of Honduran military walked past on the trail. Translucent time enveloped me. I could see the colors and expressions in their eyes and I judged the guilty and the innocent as they filed past.

They never noticed my reclining body, although they looked right at me: absent within their ordered voyage, minding their own footsteps and then vanishing through a slit in the green curtain.

The jungle can sometimes be like the surface of a blind mirror and invisible things live and breathe there.

I am in my hut and Stanley comes to tell me there is a big meeting at the office. A very important person is visiting and they want me there. "Who is it?" I ask.

"Don't know," says Stanley.

Maritxu is asleep in a hammock. I touch her long black hair goodbye and go out the door. She has been having nightmares lately, recalling the torture she received at the vile hands of the Spanish government.

When I get to the main building the Honduran colonel is talking to a contingent of U.S. Embassy people who normally aren't around. The radio operator is busy with the incoming helicopter pilot, telling him about the weather and the landing zone.

The rainforest grows all around the camp and today it is on its best behavior. There is no rain and the visibility is great. I hear the radio operator give a 5 by 5 call back and then one of the embassy guys pulls me over and tells me that they want me to talk informally to the Nobel Peace Prize winner who is about to land. "He's on the helicopter and you are the only one here right now, so you've got to step up."

"No problem," I say, but of course, there is a problem and I find out about it a few days later.

The Nobel Peace Prize winner is surrounded by a contingent of people who appear to be from the inner circle of a revolutionary council. The women are severe and they tightly grip brief cases. The men are bald with intense eyes surrounded by fragile, wire rimmed glasses that look like they are going to break at any moment. The entire group is seething and suspicious.

The Nobel Peace Prize winner is different. He is tall and elegant, dressed in a safari jacket and low cut boots and he could easily pass for an older model in a magazine spread advertising outdoor fashion.

His silver hair could sell anything and his smile is brilliant. On closer inspection I can see why he has won the Peace Prize; his eyes disappear into a dark pain somewhere in the past. He is highly political and a torture victim.

The embassy staff and colonel take him into a meeting room and conduct a briefing about the situation of the refugees. After it is over, they introduced me. I am to take him into one of the nearby villages that the U.N. has constructed as part of a resettlement program.

When we arrive at the village the Nobel Peace Prize winner begins to speak to the refugees. An incident along the border comes up. We had received a radio message the day before that the Sandinistas had attacked a border village and killed eleven Honduran Indians. I confirm to the Nobel Peace Prize winner that yes, the radio message had been received.

He takes this news like his mother has just died. From that moment on, until I watch his helicopter lift off, it looks as if his mind is trapped inside a late-night library, poring over ancient documents and recent cables, trying to find the missing information to complete his massive book on jungle politics.

Two days later, the Nobel Peace Prize winner holds a news conference in the Nicaraguan capital of Managua. In the newspaper photo the Sandinistas wear grim faces. He states that during his visit to the border, he has uncovered information that the Honduran military has attacked a village inside Nicaragua and killed eleven Nicaraguans. Further, he says, the American CIA is involved in the massacre.

My name is mentioned by someone as the source of this information.

I guess I was never very good at big time politics. I was much too interested in how the river made its white-way toward the sea or how the neon told stories in dark bars or how the tortured girl in my bed muttered in her dreams. A natural religion of how people lived and died and the tale of animals feasted upon their own were much closer to my heart than the politics of men with guns and their fight to control the surface of the planet.

Maybe the radio message was a plant or real, or perhaps the Nobel Peace Prize winner was actually correct. I never found out: the political bullshit was more opaque than the jungle.

Of course, the Nobel Peace Prize winner really didn't know me. I think he would have been surprised to learn of my wildly left-leaning, atheistic politics and to meet Maritxu. They could have discussed mutual torture and we could have toasted the ideal of world revolution and the defeat of the Contras.

In all though, it was interesting to see my name in the print of communist media and then sitting through endless meetings at the U.S. Embassy. I got to know the political staff quite well and none of them liked me. A few thought I was a complete fucking idiot, but the feeling was shared and we tried to act innocent and smart as we stared at each other over the smooth divide of the ambassador's long brown table.

A man gave me an old, used bag in Bangkok on the steps of the President's Hotel. I carried it for years. The bag was purchased in 1965 at Clark's Coats of New York City. The lock opened by dialing 6969. The man who gave it to me was tall, thin, had curly black hair, was a sex addict, and intimidated people with eyebrows that looked like knives. Some people thought he was a spy, but I thought he was one of the greatest writers to have every lived. He had apparently been taking speed mixed with Meyer's Rum for a few days and the words he spoke were electric and rapid. Although later, he denied drug use and said his metabolism was naturally out of control. You could get sunburned standing too close to the guy. He seemed surprised when I recognized him. Shit man, you're a star. Hollywood loves you. A few years later he killed himself with another kind of bag. I still have the bag he gave me. It talks at night. The voice is persistent, cogent. For the bag, things are open or shut, light or dark, right or wrong, dead stopped or moving at 1,000 miles per hour. Life for the bag is a long dream in mostly rough weather. Someday, someone will find the tattered bag and toss it into the garbage, not realizing that it is part of the long, literary tradition of refugees. Not understanding that common things can possess uncommon people and cause explosions of creativity.

GUATEMALA

THE EYES OF MAN AND DOG

HE DECIDED to drink himself to death. He told me so when I had given him a few quetzals. "Buy some food for yourself and your dog," I said. "You can always die later. If you go, the dog's got nothing. You wouldn't want that, would you?"

The ghost of a racing Whippet followed him everywhere with devout brown eyes and a badly scarred nose caused by a starting gate. A few of the sober locals told me she had been one of the best and she ran like a child's rocking horse come to life, but she really didn't run. She floated, never touching the earth.

Her name was Laica and she probably had cancer. Her name meant outside the church and from the bone looks of her, beyond god.

My words didn't matter. All of his begged quetzals went to buying rubbing alcohol and little bottles of aguardente that he mixed into a nice flavor. Where most people had white in the eyeball, he had a red and black shiny surface that looked like liquid from a cenote; the deep limestone water caverns where priests used to throw jade studded children and bloody hearts.

His eyes were filled with the antiquity of Guatemala and you could see him drowning in there, asking for a few more centavos to hang onto as he sank to the bottom. He quit buying food for Laica and himself and then he started to get really sick and the dog began to dissolve into the sprints of her past.

Covered in dirt and vomit the dying drunk would sit in the park passed out with Laica by his side. They warmed each other in the cold mountain air and she made the most of loving him. He used to be a human being. Now he was a piece of guttural history that kept falling down on sidewalks, moaning universal lessons for uniformed school children as they marched along with standard steps.

As I approached him one day, he had gathered a little crowd around him. Laica was there looking into the faces. He was showing off the burn on his leg. It looked awful. He'd been cooking on a little bucket and somehow his leg had caught fire. He pulled on some black, dead skin and I told him to quit drinking rubbing alcohol and put it on the leg. He just laughed at me.

A few days later, I found him dead under a tree. He reminded me of the other lifeless forms that occupied the glass tombstone in my brain. Breath had left him on his own. His head lay back across the contorted roots of the old tree with his eyes and mouth wide open. Pieces of rags and crushed paper lay around like the empty words of his passing.

Laica was also there, mad with hunger and she started to follow me thinking I had food. I took her up the park to a woman who sold chicken. I bought a whole raw bird and threw it down. Laica looked at me in disbelief, but then she fell upon the meat with her waning power.

We returned to where the drunk had died beneath the tree. The garbage collector had alerted the police and some sort of official pick-up was just arriving. As I continued my morning stroll, I imagined the dead beggar and his truthful dog taking the elevator up through the floors of my glass tombstone to the big penthouse; the one that overlooked the whole wide world of my clinging, clawing disaster.

Laica stayed behind as they loaded the body into the ambulance and then she headed into the park, but she kept stopping to look back in despair at the long troubled past of dogs and the poor bastards who petted them while begging money for booze.

It was a kind of sad relationship that bordered on love and I guess I could recognize it pretty well.

Pressure was in the room. The admiral and I were cooking. My heart rate was up. He and I had grown close. I would quote Mao to him and he gave me lines from Alfred Thayer Mahan. We sat at a round table inside the International Policy Institute in good old Washington, D.C. We had worked together on interdicting Cubans and Haitians who were trying to swim across the Gulf of Mexico to America. It was a long swim. The U.S. Navy was picking them up and dumping them in Guantanamo, but the place was busting at the seams, so the drug infested country of Panama had kindly agreed to store some of them in the Panama Canal Zone: for money, of course. I'd help to set up camps, put in services. I was a civilian on the general staff. We had been called to Washington to receive a thank-you; give a briefing at one of the regular meetings of the Institute. In the room were two ex-senators, an ex-representative, an ex-judge, an ex-head of the CIA, and some working stiff policy wonks. We were both listening, looking at each other sideways, waiting. I was sure I was going to keel over as the meeting droned. I did whorehouses and bars better than institutes and then I noticed that the admiral had a small bead of sweat dribbling down his temple. This was the opening I was looking for and instead of waiting to be introduced by the guy chairing the meeting, I interrupted him and said that the admiral and I had an upcoming appointment at the Eisenhower Executive Office Building and could we please just say a word right now? The room went silent and then the guy said sure, go ahead. I gave a glowing report on the admiral and then he gave a glowing report on me and then we got up and left. The lie about the Executive Office Building followed us all the way to a Georgetown bar and we sat with a bunch of drunken college students and for the first time that day, we were happy in the national capital of our superpower country.

KENYA

DEATH SPREADS HER LEGS

DEATH CAN STIMULATE ME sexually. The first time I noticed it was when I attended a funeral for two people. This was double the fun and somebody was saving on expenses. The people in the boxes up at the front had been executed like a couple of pigs. The eulogies seemed pointless to me. They were hollow words and could not compete with the real images of my two lost friends.

I watched them as they stood with sacks over their heads, hands tied, mouths taped and then a small man shoved them onto the sand. It was a lonely little spot far from the cooling moon, close to the burning sun.

A knife came out and down it went into the hearts, slowly pushing through the skin, short little strokes, back and forth like slicing a Christmas ham.

Why waste two bullets?

Nobody was talking about those kinds of things? That was information we could all use, but no, we were knee deep in the Bible and feel-good lies told by people who knew very little about the living or the dead.

I was listening to testimonials about how the girl was a "simple person, a kind person" and that the man loved "politics and dogs." I wanted to shout that "Hey, lady, we all love dogs!" but I didn't, since I thought that maybe there were some cat people in the room.

I dozed off inside my mind. I went through the weather systems and over the mountains to where my friends lay twisting upon the ground in their unique last moments. It could just as easily been me, but it wasn't. I was sitting here looking at all the people who had come to be part of whatever the fuck this was.

The sermon went silent and open mouths moved without words as I glowed a thousand miles away. As I was visualizing all of this my penis started to harden, not in a noticeable way, but just sort of moving around in my pants. I shifted in my seat and noticed a girl on my aisle. She had on a tight dress.

Why would she wear a tight dress to a funeral?

I think it helps to know the dead. Otherwise, it is hard to identify with them in the way that I am talking about, in a manner that causes one to become sexually excited. When the dead are anonymous, that is something else and outside the scope of this scholarly paper.

I am unsure if this is a natural reaction or if I am an abnormal case. I don't know and really don't care. Reactions to life and death are pretty much all we have and I need to be happy with who I am, since there is no alternative.

When I got home, I tackled Teresa at the door and shoved her back down the hall to our "safe room" with bars on the windows and doors. She struggled with me and told me to calm down. She went into the bathroom and came out naked. I turned on the overhead fan and lay beneath the moving air looking at her beach volleyball body.

We began to make love in honor of my friends. Teresa didn't know. I never told her, but the funeral was continuing in our bed and that was when I noticed sex and death sitting there.

Death blew his breath upon me from the lungs of my friends. Sex wrapped her mouth around my penis from all the oral stimulation that either one of them had ever experienced.

I felt like an old elephant saying goodbye to cherished, lifeless forms on the trail.

I orgazmed as sex and death looked on.

We took a break and I went into the kitchen to eat a sandwich. My two dogs followed me. Do dogs know when we are naked? They seem to care.

Later that night when Teresa and I lay together in bed I reached for her from a deep hole that sex and death had dug. I tried to climb out. She looked down at me from the edge.

Teresa placed her hand on mine and slowly smoothed my skin and pressed my fingers together. Her hand wrote comforting words across my skin and she spelled our names.

Sex and death lay there with us on the bed. The dogs snuggled next to them and outside I heard a drunken group of party animals calling for all of us to get up and put on our clothes. They were in a taxi and heading downtown to a new restaurant that had a great reggae band.

Teresa said she was sleepy. I begged off and watched sex and death walk outside and get into the vehicle. They looked like stained glass. I thought to myself, well they are going to have a good time. I could see them eating, drinking and dancing with sparks flying off their feet. People were going to applaud as they did turns on the floor that drilled into the foundation and compromised the basic structure of the building.

I guess the party went too far. I read a society column in the newspaper the next morning. The writer had spotted them at the restaurant making a big scene and they had gotten into trouble. The manager had asked death to leave and sex threw a fit. The police were called and both of them had been arrested.

I was a little surprised, but as I thought about sex and death, it all seemed to make sense. Those two mysteries were more than we could ever be and they lived in a vast space that science had only barely begun to clean.

I finished breakfast and began to prepare for a new day. I was going to walk and talk with the living. I also expected the dead to be on the edges, breathing ice down my neck: nothing more to do.

What of sex? Well, as I drove to work a typical sexual feeling soon entered my mind. I spotted a shapely girl standing at a bus stop. Her breasts were playing tennis with the passing cars. Men looked back at her, allowing the cars to drive themselves. She had nothing to do with death and for that I was happy as I watched her stroke another fuzzy ball just inside the service box.

She waits at her kitchen table for nothing. The passing moments keep her company and they glide in front of her face, leaving a faraway glaze upon her eyes. Most of her family is underground and her brother is in jail. Governments have come and gone, but still her name waits on a list of expected state enemies like a door forced at night. She volunteers at the prison where she used to be part of the population. Sometimes she takes out old photos and finds a young, beautiful woman riding in a boat on the water of a lagoon. The sun is breaking under a low cloud and showering the jungle with gold coins. The smell of the boat and the Indians and the feel of the mud and the river come over her.

All of those moments are lost now, down the bottles and up all night and into the long walks by the sea. If we could return to the past, what would we regain? Don't we all need a second chance, another moment to hold what we have lost? She considers these thoughts and then goes into her bedroom and lies down. My shoes are horses she says out loud and then laughs. On her bedside table is an assortment of pills. Her stomach is bad and she is smoking too much and drinking large amounts of coffee and wine, but then there is little else and anyway, she is a torture survivor and that can go a long way in justifying bad habits and creating endless nights. She lights a cigarette and the spreading smoke becomes her coughing soul. Love gone wrong burns a chain of cigarettes and then she leaves her little apartment and walks down to the docks, where she watches the lights move on the water and she waits there for hours, as the past slowly destroys the present. She reaches into the air and pulls down a useless creature and places it firmly on her face.

WEST HOLLYWOOD

THE HORSE LOVING REFUGEE POET OF HOLLYWOOD

I WAS BETWEEN COUNTRIES and it hurt.

The purpose of the L.A. trip was to write a screenplay. My main problem was I had never written anything. I liked to read, but reading was not writing. The process of opening my eyes seemed a bit lazier than actually moving my fingers and hands across a keyboard. What was more, the words I wrote would need to be interesting to others. The whole thing seemed fraught with indignity and waste.

My old friend told me not to worry. "Only a few people can write out here. Just look at all the shit that gets produced."

He said we could hang out at the beach and visit his haunts where Hollywood cut Vine and maybe between the parties and the bars we could come up with something. All of that sounded good, but I kept wondering why I should write and if I had what it took to be a good writer.

Hollywood and Vine got to be friendly with me. The impersonators and mourners of dead stars walked around in a constant state of Halloween. The people of Hollywood should be thankful for Halloween; it is their big orange life preserver in a sea of meaningless days. Without it most of them would drown.

One night I sat on the curb with George Sanders. He had written arguably the best suicide note ever to come out of Hollywood. Sanders had been sick, old, and probably feeling inadequate due to the young Mexican woman he was trying to make it with. She had been a minor actor in Mexico, starring in a movie adaptation of B. Traven short stories.

In the end, boredom pulled the covers back on a bed and then no one bothered to wake him and things just went on around him like nothing had happened, except he was dead; lying there naked in the breeze of the ceiling fan.

Whoever was beneath the makeup and tailored clothes looked exactly like Sanders and acted just as bored. He offered me a hit off a joint. He gestured toward a bunch of street kids hanging nearby and said, "I used to be like that. Now I have a reason to live."

I'd take long turns alone, up and down the streets of Hollywood. I'd meet parents putting up posters of their missing kids on street lamps and telephone poles.

Some of the people I met were refugees. We talked about how their kids were having hard times coping with all the change, how the trip to America on the boats and through the jungle and across the borders had fucked them up.

The posters showed plenty of white American types, but also Vietnamese, Cambodians, and Salvadorans, running from war or death squads or pimps. The eyes of the children were like deep wells that only had a tiny glint somewhere down there, way past the damp walls where the light waves journeyed.

The photos of the kids on the posters turned as I walked by. The expressions followed after me whispering trash. After a few minutes they'd grow tired of me and float up into the leaves and brush of the foothills. Deep in a canyon a hidden hole would attract them and they'd hang in the air. Winter would come and then spring and the wild flowers would pop out and finally the hovering faces that had followed me months before would curl up like dogs at the base of a tree and go to sleep.

There was one big draw in my effort to write a script. My friend had a pointed, beautiful blonde agent who drove a 1973 MG Midget and was eager to read our script. She thought that between my friend's feel for dialogue and my colorful stories we might produce a saleable product.

Her white, straight teeth were very positive.

A few minutes after we met, I didn't like her. I watched as she torched a guy at the buffet table. He made a fairly decent pass at her and she said that she knew him and then he said, "No, I don't think we've met." She smiled, "Oh yeah, I know you. I know you very well." Her eyes stuck him like knives in a gutted pig and he stood there on fire while people holding drinks held out a free hand to get warm.

The agent had gotten my friend some T.V. guest spots and under-fives and to his credit he had scored a couple of major movie roles. Things were looking up for him, so the whole venture, at least from his side, seemed like it might work. I had my doubts and should things collapse my backup plan was to meet an aging star and be held captive in sad luxury for a few months.

I kept practicing the line: "I write, I act, I sing, but what I do best is direct." I felt women of all stripes would feel obligated to find out, in an intimate sort of way, if any of it was true. Of course none of it was, but in a place like L.A. that sort of a comment seemed like the truth when compared to the giant deceptions that stomped the streets crushing buses and turning smiles upside down.

A complication to the plan was that my old friend had married my old girlfriend. I was unsure how that would work out, but within a few days I realized none of us remembered much about the way it had been. We vaguely recalled El Salvador and laughed about how some people suspected a ménage a trois.

Men are not to my taste. I find women far more infuriating and worthy of my effort. I like the smoothness of women even when they are draining my spirit and filling expensive glass flutes with genetic liquid that used to be me.

So I moved into my threesome friend's old stucco fourplex on a side street in West Hollywood. The other tenants were a family that had a convicted child molester, a Vietnam War vet and his gorgeous, loose wife, and a quiet Muslim man who had a way of squeezing religion out of his beard.

I went out my first night there. Luck led me to sitting naked across from a like-minded girl who had the same birthday as me. We had met at a Sunset bar when I heard her quoting Baudelaire and now we were intertwined; legs and arms dropping over each other like warm California waterfalls.

She was a rich, half-French refugee from Vietnam. Her father and mother had been ground up in the slaughterhouse politics of South Vietnam in the early 1970's. They had placed a bad bet on Nguyen Cao Ky and ended up being blown to bits compliments of a car bomb rigged by shadowy hands.

At the time of the explosion, the girl was studying French poetry at the Sorbonne and although her fat bank account stopped receiving automatic deposits she still had enough to tide her over into the next century. She arrived in the United States with good recommendations, a four-star document from the U.S. Embassy in Paris granting her political refugee status, and a fellowship at the University of Southern California.

These were the days of U.S. buyer's regret as we tried to salvage some sort of forgiveness for our sins in Vietnam; she was blessed due to that old standby, American stupidity.

She had spent the last eight years or so trying way too hard to become a cool American chick. On many fronts she had made it.

She was a full-time poet and part-time screenplay writer with beauty, intelligence, language fluency, a racehorse, and a lot of money. It was the perfect combination for Hollywood, but then something happened. Eventually, she would jump out of a moving car on the I-10. She had been on the passenger side and was having an animated discussion with her boyfriend about horses and infidelity. Nobody could recognize her after she stopped skidding and the traffic was snarled past midnight.

Her poetry, I guess, had become too true with nothing left to hang onto. Still, I can think of better ways to end a conversation, even a last conversation.

We talked about the movies. During her first few years in town she had written a few scripts that nobody read. Her friends in the business had been on the sleazy side and she eventually gave up the movies for poetry.

Words bounced out of her mouth like tennis balls. Character and meter and agents and dirty deals and unfortunate blow jobs were being picked up at the net by adolescents in shorts. I understood everything she spat out since the Captigons and wine we were downing had turned convoluted ideas into prize winners.

We told each other we were going to be famous someday as long as we didn't get killed getting there. We agreed that talk about death was tragically sexy, like James Dean looking down at us from her wall.

"Yeah, I could tell you stuff," her long difficult pause came at the expense of her lips. She told me a few Hollywood clichés that were like that because they were true; about lowlifes in good clothes and how radioactive half-lies were poisoning her.

"I get these subtle visions in the oddest places," she said. "They come floating on someone's face or in the tone of a voice. Missed appointments, nobody picking up. Typical. When you don't get the joke, you're in trouble. You get cut all the time around here. It's like the stigmata."

"You know why people write?" she sighed.

Finally, here it was: a sign.

"No, enlighten me," I said. "Well for starters we're all telling the same story. It's just that some of us make money from the story. I mean who'd write for free?"

"I don't know. Emily Dickinson."

"She's different. There's always the exception. Anyway, she died in the corner of a locked room. That's not the life I want. Things change, you know?"

"Yeah, I guess neither of us is Emily Dickinson."

"Right," and then she began.

I can't quote it exactly, but it had a smooth track-like texture and I lay my head back and gripped the accent on the side of her cultured voice. The ride was fast and went something like this: I know you, but you are only secondary, since this story is all about me. I lived all of this more or less and it is sad and about now, the past, the future, things that explode, giving up and giving in, worms, poison, sleeping, kids, ghosts, gold, spinning objects in space, arguing, getting high, dogs and cats, repression, lust, killing strangers, laughing, broken dreams, alibis, taking stuff from people, abnormal existence, stars, one celled organisms marching through time, doing stuff, money, monsters, life, death, and nothing. My writing is meant to invade your real life. I am the occupying mind and I shall build my kingdom in your body and post soldiers and whores of myself all along your vital signs charging money and questioning your thoughts. Eventually a little piece of you will become me. After all, you are undeveloped and smelly and do wicked things, but once you read my words some of that will change, you will learn from me, and you will pay me for the benefits that my thoughts will bring to you.

"I'm going to make money from my poetry. I want to be the resident poet at a good university. I'd like that. I could keep horses near my cottage. I'm sentimental you see."

She read me her poems. They all started out with hope and ended in tragedy as if her words were totally resigned to a fallen utopia. Loss was her currency; I could see it in her eyes. Black holes were the main image. She was always drawn into them, unable to see, forced to feel along the dense, unhappy gravity that paralyzed her. Other people were vague plastic dreams she kept at arm's distance. In her poetic world, only she could sense as she ran her fingers over the forms of manikins and substitute people who moved dead-footed and dull through her life.

I would have given her the Nobel Prize had I had one in my pocket.

"I really would like to believe in someone; a man maybe, a lover. Would you like to write something in my notebook?" she said.

And so I wrote that rain is a religion and death is only hearsay and the dust of missing kids rises on the wind to settle upon freeway traffic and the children of Hollywood hitchhike down to the coast in search of orations in the sand. I finished by saying that attractive women in bikinis washing dirty cars in Venice reminded me of funerals for missing children, particularly after the rain had fallen and sanctified the surface of the cars and blessed the soapy run off.

We stayed up all that night and most of the next day. Anonymous, long distance looks finally replaced our desultory conversation and we made a certain kind of love as if no trace of us could ever be found by men in rubber suits working for the county. We were missing, even to ourselves.

I left her asleep on the floor of her apartment. She was dreaming of horses. I knew by the way her hair lay straight out behind her on the carpet, like she was riding a smart horse across the countryside and the wind was trying to steal her away.

As I walked toward my place in West Hollywood, the cool air seemed full of possibilities. The early morning light was like a shining appointment with somebody important.

I thought about what she said about writing. Maybe you could make money from it, even if it was poetry. Sure, people would pay you for the words that came out of your brain and if poetry was a college salary, then a screenplay was like an executive cash register. So a few days later I started working on a movie with my old friend. We titled it, "Living and Dying with Dogs".

It was about the end of the world and it was going to make us rich.

I saw it as a comedy. We eventually finished it and nobody liked it, not even the bitchy blonde agent, but people did steal from it. Two years later a medium budget movie with wide release and a couple major stars somehow ended up with six of our plot points. It was an old story and the movie made everybody money, except the two people who wrote the fucking thing.

My old friend and I eventually got cross with each other when we tried to turn the movie into a play, but even after our words had come between us, he still bothered to call and tell me the details of how the refugee horse lover poet had jumped to her death. His voice was a distant echo from our self-centered past.

They were rolling at around 70 miles per hour towards the beach in the rain at night. Her boyfriend had said he was screwing someone else. He thought it okay to tell her then, but he guessed wrong, because there had been something unseen in the car, something missed after all the times he had made love to her and talked her down from her highs and gotten her up from her lows, after all of that, he still overlooked the fact that she couldn't take another loss, even a chicken shit one, like an unfaithful boyfriend.

He had overlooked the idea of poetic spontaneity and how the process is one of subtraction, not addition. Loss is a way to build. Subtraction for her, as for all the great poets, is more a disease than a math operation. The final removal, of course, is you and that was the last line she edited on the I-10.

Missing her meds hadn't helped either.

I asked him if there had been any murdered street kids clinging to the car or had the police found a utopia spreading out from her body. He said he didn't know what the fuck I was talking about and hung up.

I never spoke to him again, nor did I ever go back to Hollywood. I was done with all of that. It was time to move on to bigger things, like Afghanistan and the death of a million people.

Billy checked his watch; it was midnight and soon they would cross. We were sitting in our vehicle just above the main Ruzizi bridge on the Rwandan side. William Potter Pilgrim was his Australian name and he was my key aide in this massive human disaster. Somehow my agency had found him. His resume read like a long drunken lie. Among other things he was ex-French Foreign Legion and had been part of a search and destroy contingent that the French used to track down smugglers, kidnappers, killers, and other bastards that attacked their friends and allies on the African continent. The big plus was he had trained most of the Zaire paratroopers who now controlled the shadowy bridge we were looking at. He was a nervous man and we drank together like hellions from below and I liked him in that yes, I keep poisonous snakes in my room sort of way. One night he stripped down and fired his automatic weapon into the house where his expat lover slept, but all of that was a coming attraction about PTSD and alcoholism. The Rwandan Patriotic Army Captain had visited us a few days before. He was trying to locate three men who had organized the slaughter of several thousand people at the soccer stadium where my logistics team had established a base camp. We had taken over the place from the French military that had pulled out into the Green Zone. Billy had contacted his Mobutu paratroop buddies and they had found the three people the RPA wanted. It didn't take much and Billy had arranged the whole thing. So here we sat waiting. This was a small affair and I thought that maybe in the big wash of things it was a good deed. We had found hundreds of bodies near the stadium and the whole thing was in keeping with the nightmare that we were living. I'd checked my ethics at the door when I entered the country and Billy and I were exchanging pleasantries and a pint as we watched the three men walk across the bridge with their hands tied and then thrown into the back of a truck. They're cooked said Billy. I figured they deserved the oven and now we had a huge favor that the RPA was more or less obligated to return. Somehow it all seemed okay as we headed back to the stadium that we shared with the thousands of clubbed to death Tutsi ghosts that wandered near the goals.

LAOS

EATING BREAKFAST IN THE THIRD WORLD

I AM VERSED IN THE WAYS of assholes. I am authorized to give out licenses and permits concerning them. My rubber stamp has a special seal on it that looks a bit like someone's butt sticking out the back window of a sedan trailing engine smoke down the highway.

Assholes are everywhere and when they start to do what it is that they do, they act like you are nobody. Women sometimes confuse me for one. The art of nomenclature is subtle. People can interpret glances and words and expressions anyway they want. "You fucking asshole!" is hurled at both the good and the bad. It knows no limit other than the way you feel as you contemplate the person in front of you.

My classification is more along the lines of detached and cold. Similar to the happy Captain of an icebreaker on long term duty in the Arctic who finds himself trapped in the ice. That doesn't seem to me like an asshole; just somebody who has a unique perspective and nowhere to go. That's me: trapped on my island, isolated, talking to myself, and enjoying it. You'd be surprised how many people dislike you for that.

Two Frenchmen were eating breakfast in the Third World. They didn't speak the local language, but both were conversant in English. Most of the locals who worked in restaurants for foreigners could also speak a little English. The French language had gone down the toilet a few years earlier due to too many dead Frenchmen lying around the countryside. The same could be said of the Americans, but for some reason, English was hanging in there. Of course, the biggest body count was local, but nobody cared about that language.

I was a few tables away ordering my food. I peppered my English with a few native phrases. The waiter brought me a plate full of stuff I had not ordered. I told him I couldn't eat it. The Frenchmen were eating the same food and looked at me like I was a sick animal in a zoo.

The waiter apologized and brought me what I had ordered. I assumed he had spit in it. As he was walking away one of the Frenchmen said, "You ordered what he brought you the first time."

When I looked over at him I imagined Charles De Gaulle's nose. The reference dates me. Most people don't know who Charles De Gaulle is, much less what his nose looked like, but he is the man who made France what it is today. He hated most Frenchmen almost as much as he hated the British, the Americans, the Russians, the Italians, and, of course, the Germans.

I think he pretty much hated everything except his nose. He loved his nose as he stuck the pride of France into every corner of the world. You can't get away from the De Gaulle nose. His sniff put a lot of people to shame. I think it was why he finally defeated all his enemies and took over the country. With a nose like that he could have been a great clown, but he chose to be a great leader instead.

As De Gaulle grew older and wiser and more powerful, so did his nose.

I didn't respond and kept eating my food. As I sat there I was reminded of the time I was walking along a beach in another country where languages had been crushed together by marching armies. I passed a little girl who was playing in the sand. She was as red as a shiny Washington apple. The parents were sitting there drinking beer and I said in broken English mixed with a tonal dialect of some sort, "I don't know if you noticed, but your little girl is really getting sunburned." The man said in accented English, "Fuck off."

I decided that the Frenchman rebuking me over my food order was a very similar situation, except this time nobody was saying, "Fuck off."

I am patient with Frenchmen, not French women. I can hardly wait for them to show up. No, Frenchmen have had a hard time with German men, like children trying to picnic in the midst of a landslide. It has put them into a century long tailspin. The men of France have taken shelter behind absurdist walls that are more comforting than the Maginot Line.

France should thank the likes of Sartre and Camus every day. They have given all Frenchmen the right to say, "Nothing matters." They are right, of course, but not in the way they think.

I left my money on the table and as I passed the Frenchmen I gave them, in perfect German, the punch line to an old joke: "Thanks for the shade on the Champs-Elysees. Our boys loved it."

My mother was born in Alsace-Lorraine so I figured I could give them a ribbing under the circumstances, what with my bloodline having been ripped to shreds by the warring armies of France and Germany.

I knew that this little incident would stay with me for many years. That is the way things work in the Third World of breakfast. You never know what haughty, great leader you might meet over your fish sauce.

Hanzila was accompanied by six young men. She had handed Iggi the can of gasoline. He kicked open the door and went inside. He splashed the gasoline across the people lying on the floor. One of the little boys jumped up and ran outside. Hanzila hit him in the head with her machete and he fell. Iggi closed the door and held it. One of the other boys broke a window and tossed a lit book of matches inside. The room of the school house was very small and the fire jumped up to the windows. They listened to them scream and crash around inside for a few seconds and then Iggi opened the door. A few of them staggered out and were quickly cut down. Hanzila and the others watched them burn on the ground. They all agreed it was beautiful to watch ancient revenge twist and smoke. God approved of the whole thing and they sang a perverted hymn on their way back to the bar.

ZAIRE

SHE SAW JESUS STANDING THERE

HANZILA LAY ON CARDBOARD with her child and two beaten dogs in a small alley just off the main road leading to the airport. Imanna, the old false god, fought an army of angels high over her head. Archangel Michael swung his machete and with every blow Satan's blood splashed across the clouds.

Her glazed eyes watched the battle as she strained to breathe. The apocalypse was here in vivid red colors and the recent past of genocide and war and cholera, although clutching at her, seemed unimportant.

The two dogs were thin, exhausted and dying at her feet. They had a better sense than the woman about what was happening. Hunger had given way to the internal scent of death and they began to long for a quiet, cool, dark spot. Their instincts were free of politics and religion and all the lies perpetuated by humans. The dog world was more basic and immediate. They lived in that cut-bone truth that humans had lost long ago.

The Goma airport roared with activity. The sounds of airplanes landing were foreign to her. She had only seen them high in the sky and didn't believe what people said about them. A few days ago, as she walked toward the alley of her future, the noise of the engines surprised her since she thought airplanes only moved silently.

Sometimes when she watched the planes she thought they flew just like the white Jesus when he rose into the sky above Jerusalem.

Hutu Catholicism had come easily to Hanzila and she lay in the alley with her sick child, waiting for Jesus to save both of them. She knew he would forgive her sins. Killing the children and burning the women and bashing in the skulls of so many were not things beyond redemption. One needed only to believe.

Her heart beat like a good colonial clock and she counted down the time. Suddenly she became excited. She grabbed one of the dogs by the ears and it squealed and then in her old Hutu dialect she yelled, "I am ready. Take us with you. My child is innocent!"

Her shouting grew louder as she tried to get the attention of Jesus and one of his disciples standing at the end of the alley. They were drinking holy water that looked a lot like beer.

I picked up my assistant at the airport. He had come in on a Luftwaffe cargo plane. The irony of flying staff in on the air force built by the Nazis seemed ironic and slightly wrong, but tools had no emotional history. He was from Maine and this was his second tour of Africa. The cholera epidemic was raging. He kept asking me questions and then I said let's stop in here, they have the only cold beer in town. As we stood drinking on the sidewalk he asked what is that woman saying? She was down at the end of the alley with a child and two dogs. I told him I had no idea, but I could tell she was in the last stages of her cholera and she would probably be dead soon. He frowned and said she looks really sick and so does her kid. We need to help them. I told him we didn't have time and that this scene was being repeated by the thousands all over the place. Our job at that moment was to drive out of town and try to find a convoy of trucks that was coming from Nairobi. I had gotten a radio message that they were stuck at the border. No we can't leave them he said. I was beginning to worry about this guy. Look, I replied I understand how you feel, but you just got here. Stick with me today and try to tamp down your first impressions and by tonight you'll understand. He looked at me and walked down to where the woman was shouting. I touched his arm and said we had to go and he followed me back to the vehicle and we left her there to die with her kid and two dogs. She was screaming. The last things I saw when we drove away were the looks of shock and anger on her face. Her dogs were motionless; dead in the alley at the woman's feet like a pair of door stops keeping the gates open for the rest of us.

THAILAND

THE BUS AT THE END
OF MY UNIVERSE

I'D COME OUT OF THE HILLS every six weeks or so in a kind of lawless daze known only to those who by choice live in refugee camps. It was a condition that replaced professionalism with dread.

Instead of looking like I could handle anything that came my way, I had the appearance of a victim, even though I wasn't one, at least not in the same sense as those around me.

Of course in my case having recurrent malaria caused people to be confused when they saw my face, my eyes. Malaria leaves burn marks on your expressions that others don't recognize You start to look like black paint has turned your eyeballs into a gallery show and the reviews are bad: "All those horrible, dark images. I had to flee."

My female partners worried I was losing interest in them, that perhaps I was turning gay or blasé. No, I'd say, it was only the aftermath of malaria triggering those kinds of features when I couldn't come. It was the dregs of malaria glazing my eyes as I'd watch my lovers take bucket baths.

My dead glances caused recriminations to spring from the mouths of women like wet, underfed cats. Something was not right about my explanations. No one believed me.

The side of my face reflected on the window close to the little red dot of the setting sun as the driver gunned the engine and we swung onto the highway. The night bus was almost empty and I was way in the back: a good place to be when shrouded in misery. My only relief was going to be the soft blue valium rolling between my thumb and forefinger.

I was leaving the camp for a few days, going against the mad cadence of my leaping shaman. "Don't travel on the bus right now! The veins in the chicken skull are lousy with purple. Monsters are waiting for you. They know your name!"

After a few cups of homebrewed gasoline, I'd left the screaming shaman's hut at the top of the hill and wound my way down the narrow path through the sparkle of ten thousand refugee fires.

His worm eaten dogs trailed my steps like disappointed friends. Their thoughts climbed the hairs on the back of my neck and entered into my ears. They questioned my choices. I heard their dog voices say, "You need to believe the guy who feeds us. He's some kind of god or something."

Maybe the shaman and his dogs were right. Maybe the signs were untouchably bad, but I had to get out of the camp, even if it did kill me.

Our camp was at the center of the universe where time began and ended. It was the place where we lived and sometimes laughed with our old pal death. We saw the bugger on a daily basis and when you are young and inexperienced, you have to wing it with death; you have to try things out, find something that works.

Everybody was different in how they handled it. I decided to make death my demented friend, my criminal partner. Death told me I was full of shit every so often and after I'd left angry, he'd steal everything out of my room and sell it cut rate to rich refugees and then blow the money on imported cheese and cheap booze and throw insane parties that burned hot, red holes into the blackness of the night: parties that I attended despite my hurt feelings.

I'd sit silently in the corner watching people dance.

Death always brought out focused, poetic, desperate acts in all of us. Women would literally jump into my bed. They loved me and I loved them. Moments were floods of emotion and they rushed and crashed like white-capped water across bamboo beds.

The sex was always heightened when death stole from me. The intensity, I guess, was a way of paying me back for the stuff that went missing, stuff I would occasionally spot in a trader's boat or hear in the words that came from a pure heart.

As I sat in my seat on the all night bus to the capital, leaning into the risks of the jungle road, I began to nod off, comforted by the hum and cold of the air conditioner and the green glow of the marque dashboard.

The driver seemed crazed and was clearly on some sort of white-knuckle drug. I felt medical comfort knowing he had taken something to stay awake while I had popped something to put me to sleep. We all tried to extend ourselves just a little past our normal function. At 70 miles per hour on a moonless road I imagined the gods of smooth asphalt and smart water buffaloes clearing the way for our carefree passage.

About six hours from the capital I opened my eyes and felt my bag move. The heavy-duty world traveler sitting behind me had tried to get his hand into my mochila azul, the leather bag that made me look like I carried letters for a living. He was a German with dreads down to his ass that had gone north to score cheap heroin.

I told him to fuck off and instead of pulling his knife and stabbing me in the heart, he said, "Sorry, I thought I knew you. Yeah, I do know you. I know your name." I told him to fuck off again and he moved a few seats up. He had plenty to choose from.

Another dead guy I thought.

I gave a long yawn and leaned my head toward my knees. I needed to get back to sleep. But I was out of valium, and as the ride wore on, totally out of luck. My destination seemed to be receding from the oncoming bus. I worried I'd never get there. Never make it to the drunks and whores, never get to write poetry in bar books or eat cheap noodles or watch the clock tick down on another dawn.

Maybe it was just as well going backwards in a forward motion. Everything led to the end of the alley anyway; unexpected turns with no explanations except for those ultimate signs from a still night or a painting or a distant sound or chicken skulls.

It was then that I remembered the bottle in my bag and how the four parts of reality were constantly joining together, propping me up—time, electric charge, length, and mass. I felt at ease again and fumbled inside my bag for the smoothness of burned sand and the heat of old visions.

A faint voice came from somewhere to my side, "No more bets, please. No more bets." I turned my head to look, my seat rocked, the stench of the bathroom hit me, my mouth filled with Tequila, everything happening simultaneously as the German got up from his seat and moved through that infinite, beautiful space that eventually surrounds all of us.

In the dark I could barely see his knife.

High overhead a jet plane flew with the unthinking undead and they were packed into narrow seats that were training them for coffins.

I felt the blade as I struggled upward.

Dogs shone down upon me like moving shadows at the end of an alley and when my universe went out it was silent and infinite and mostly cold.

The bus kept rolling as I sat in my seat with my eyes wide open staring at the back of the seats in front of me.

The Ma-Chit station cleaners had waited about an hour before they boarded. There had been no big rush since the night bus was not scheduled to leave until later that evening. So the body sat there in the seat looking dead forward until one of the cleaners touched a shoulder. When they took the body off, there was a group of expatriates watching, waiting to head north. They were from all over the world, visiting Thailand for different reasons. There was a hardened Canadian, an optimistic Indian, three poets from Wales and South Africa, a couple of smart college students, a forlorn black-haired girl, a funny Kiwi chick, and two women of a certain age who glowed with a golden outline running along the edges of their bodies. A few of them were asked by the police to look at his face. They said they didn't know him, but in their hearts a faint recognition lingered. The Thai bus driver was only irritated because he was tired from driving all night. An autopsy was eventually performed by Doctor Boonyoung Wangpatimachi. As he was removing the brain, a gush of blood tissue fell upon the floor. It was a mess; a red splatter across the clean tile floor of the medical examiner. The microbes and spores wove their little forms through the flesh and began to read the tiny print of the sub-atomic, apocalyptic world. The bubbling words went like this: I don't believe in nihilism, or the unitary human soul, or the duality of Plato and Descartes, or the Geist of Hegel; no, I am more the atheist-Buddhist-shattered-crystal kind of guy. Each shard is a different moment of who we are; reflecting a changed person then and now, only to instantly alter into another being. It is why old friends say things like, "You know, I never really knew you." But we all know each other in two very special ways that never adjust: birth and death. Over the years I have concerned myself with the latter. I have seen it by legions. It comes violently or slowly, but come it does. The flesh goes in rivulets or fire or microscopic sounds as invisible organisms eat and pass our remains into pus and plants. Moisture becomes our new credit and we extend it all the way to the turmoil of the oceans and the seas. We might float on the wind for a while or turn white from the stripping rain or shift and lean as black meat marbled with worms, but eventually, all of us head to the endless water horizon; the long, lost dream of life and death, rising and falling, wave upon wave. We become as unseen dogs and run and snap at the surf, crashing into the water, caught by strong currents that take us out and down at dawn. At that moment, beyond the nasty limit of our names, we rejoin something we call infinity. In that place without end, we are dogs running and barking beside the sea and god spreads out into nothing. Since there was no one to claim the body, the authorities gave it to the Thai body snatchers. They took it down to the river for merit and burned it there on the banks and the children sat near the fire wondering about the farang who drifted upward in the smoke and then settled back down upon the water.

EPILOGUE: THE MAN WITH
THE GOLDEN SKINS

MOST AUTHORS WRITE on paper, but I decided a long time ago to use long scrolls of golden human skin. No one ever noticed. They were drunk or stoned, dead or dying.

They muttered my name in the night as I liquefied or maybe I'd reflect off cold retinas. I'd bake a memory before it was ready or smear passable moments on somebody's body. That usually fooled them.

When people got suspicious, I'd turn spinning heads into cheap airplane tickets and fly away, but I always took my skins. They look like thin sheets of sunlight preserved with the imprint of lined faces that are maps speaking my past.

Often the voices are deafening. They are the sounds of people I have left behind. I make little black hieroglyphic notations on the margins of the skins and eventually a story unrolls on the table of my mind.

Maintaining the skins is difficult. I keep them in a secret temperature controlled closet of my moving house, which travels on tiny rollers that rock and squeak nonstop. My body is a temple on wheels and I drape the skins on hangers like most of us keep expensive winter coats.

Sometimes I try them on to see if they still fit and often I find that I have outgrown them. Employees at community recycle stores, where people drop off used clothing, always wonder about my donations. As I leave the stores, I ignore their calls to stop. I walk rapidly with my head down and only turn around when I am out of sight.

I see some of my skins strolling around town on the backs of total strangers. They are worn by mostly young people that find fashion in injured clothes. The skins are a little ragged, but still function in their own mysterious ways.

I guess we all share the same story; it is just that we feel unique. The stories that define us are very old and communal. Their plot lines come from a common dream about who we are and they lead us along with tiny flashes from a distance. We are only vaguely aware of the light as we blunder toward our corporate fate, down at the end of the alley where the bums warm themselves by burning Bibles.

My supply of skins is dwindling. That is the way it should be. I am getting too old to cut out the outlines of human beings and store them in my cold vault. I am tired of carrying the dead on my back. It is hard for me to stomach the world anymore.

My taste runs with dogs and patterns in nature that cleanse me with wind and wet tongues. People are no longer of interest, unless they are kicking down my door or maybe totally lost on their way to whatever.

When I begin to die, please don't bother to resuscitate me. My skin can serve no good and even if you do have a place to keep it, you'd probably never wear it. My cells are too attenuated, too unconnected. People would wonder why you were trailing nonlinear threads.

I need to go buy a bottle of aged, white Mezcal. I'll have a few drinks while believing with all my heart that nothing matters, more than any of us will ever know.

You can count on it, particularly at the end.

THE END

MORE GREAT READS
FROM BOOKTROPE

Pacific Sun and Other Stories by **Cris Markos** (Short Stories) Pacific Sun and Other Stories explores the extremes of the human experience: from genocide and human trafficking to poverty and terminal illness. From Bosnia to Kentucky, these stories inflect the best and worst of the human psyche.

A Chorus of Wolves by **Alex Kimmell** (Short Stories - Horror) In an uncertain world, we grab familiar things to give security: Baseball, a local bar, a town sheriff, your dog, a nicely landscaped backyard, love... What happens when these safe havens become unsafe?

The Art of Work by **Phaye Poliakoff-Chen** (Short Stories) Darkly funny stories about chronic do-gooders who battle their way toward understanding, careening between resentment and fulfillment.

Behind the Shades: Hope Beyond Darkness by **Sheila Raye Charles and Glenn Swanson** (Personal Memoir) Being the daughter of a famous musician is not always what it seems. A story of hope beyond the darkness.

Suitcase Filled with Nails: Lessons Learned from Teaching Art in Kuwait by **Yvonne Wakefield** (Personal Memoir) Leaving behind a secure life in the Pacific Northwest, Yvonne Wakefield finds both joy and struggle in teaching art to young women in Kuwait. A colorful, true, and riveting tale of living and coping in the Middle East.

Discover more books and learn about our
new approach to publishing at **booktrope.com**.

22114023R00084

Made in the USA
San Bernardino, CA
20 June 2015